WOLVES OF THE CHAPARRAL

WOLVES
OF THE
CHAPARRAL

PAUL EVAN LEHMAN

M. EVANS
Lanham • Boulder • New York • Toronto • Plymouth, UK

Published by M. Evans
An imprint of Rowman & Littlefield
4501 Forbes Boulevard, Suite 200, Lanham, Maryland 20706
www.rowman.com

10 Thornbury Road, Plymouth PL6 7PP, United Kingdom

Distributed by National Book Network

British Library Cataloguing in Publication Information Available

Library of Congress Cataloging-in-Publication Data

The hardback edition of this book was previously cataloged by the Library of
Congress as follows:

Lehman, Paul Evan.
  Wolves of the chaparral, by Paul Evan Lehman.
    p. cm. — (An Evans novel of the West)
  PZ3.L52791 Wo PS3523.E434
  38013404

ISBN: 978-1-59077-424-3 (pbk.   )
ISBN: 978-1-59077-425-0 (electronic)

Printed in the United States of America

CONTENTS

WOLVES OF THE CHAPARRAL

CHAPTER I

LEAD MEDICINE

YOUNG Barry Weston dipped the brush in a basin of water and determinedly renewed his efforts to plaster down a shock of brown hair which a perverse Nature had definitely decided should be curly. His best efforts were useless; by the time he had subdued, by dint of much brushing and a liberal application of water, the last of the unruly locks, the first were dry and twisting in rebellion.

Barry detested these curls with all the masculinity of his nineteen years. Curls rhymed with girls, and, while quite becoming to one like, say, Barbara Dawn, were entirely out of place on the head of a man. Barry wondered a bit peevishly why he couldn't draw his hair over his forehead and brush it neatly in place like Joe, the bartender at the Silver Palace, did. Nature, he firmly believed, had given him a raw deal when it came to hirsute adornment.

As he frowned into the cracked mirror above the washstand, he was entirely unconscious of the fact that this same Nature had been extremely generous

9

with respect to the rest of him. His shoulders were broad, his waist slim, and he had to stoop slightly to look into the mirror. The face which frowned back at him, while tanned, was good to look upon. Just now it fairly shone from the scrubbing it had received.

Despairing of achieving a coiffure as faultless as that of Joe, Barry turned his attention to his scarf. It was a flaming yellow in color, and went very handsomely with the bright-blue silk shirt his mother had given him on Christmas. He knotted it carefully, then, before donning his coat, buckled about him a new and elaborate hand-tooled cartridge belt and holster. From the latter protruded the slick walnut handle of a Colt six-gun, Barry's most highly prized heritage from his father.

Pressing a carefully dusted gray Stetson over his wet locks, Barry cast a final critical look at his reflection and made his way to the living room. His mother was seated in her favorite rocking-chair, darning. She looked up at his entrance and smiled approvingly. His stepfather lowered the newspaper he was reading and glared at him over its top.

"Where you goin' all dressed up like a Christmas tree?" he asked sourly.

"Thought I'd ride over to the Cinchbuckle and see if Clement's goin' to town."

"You didn't dress up like that for Clement. You're goin' a-courtin' his sister. Better keep clear of the Cinchbuckle or you'll have Steve Moley in your hair."

"That polecat better stay away from her!" blazed Barry. "He's rotten to the core. Look at that waitress over at the café; she was crazy about him. His old man had a sweet time hushin' that up! And there's others. Steve Moley's got no right within fifty feet of a decent girl like Barbara Dawn."

"He gits lots closer than that, if what a feller hears is the truth," said the stepfather. "Don't you go stirrin' up trouble with Steve. We don't want Judge Moley down on us."

For his mother's sake Barry withheld the scornful words which trembled on his lips. This stepfather of his was craven; a weak-spined creature. Barry often believed that his mother had married him in order to have a man about the house to do the chores. Ignoring his foster parent, Barry crossed to where his mother sat and placed a hand on her shoulder.

"I'll be home early, ma; don't wait up."

She smiled at him. "I've got quite a bit of mendin' to do; I wouldn't be surprised if I was still up when you get back. If I'm not, I'll leave the back door unbarred. Be a good boy, now."

It was the admonition which followed him every time he went out. Barry patted her shoulder affectionately and stepped out on the gallery. It was dusk, and the evening wind swept the odor of sage across the range land. He caught up the showy pinto gelding and cinched his silver-mounted saddle in place. Barry was proud of that saddle; it had cost him a great deal of hard labor and self-denial. His step-father paid him a wage so small that he was ashamed to tell his mother.

By the time he reached the Cinchbuckle it was quite dark. There was a light in the living room of the big house, and he could hear the hands talking and laughing in the bunkhouse. The gallery was a recess of deep shadows. He swung from his horse at the hitch rack and ascended the steps.

"Is that you, Barry?"

He turned swiftly. Barbara was back there in the gloom. Probably in the hammock.

"You bet it's me," he said, and started to grope his way to her side.

His foot struck a riding boot extended in the darkness. Had he been moving more rapidly he would have tripped over it. As he was recovering his balance, a voice spoke drawlingly.

"Good evenin', Mister Weston."

Barry stiffened, peering at the rocking chair from which the boot extended. That was Steve Moley's voice; he was there in the shadows with Barbara.

"You, huh?" Barry grated.

"Who'd you think it was; Clement?"

A stifled laugh from Barbara forced the climax. To a girl of sixteen the awkward stumbling, followed by the dry question, was a bit of harmless by-play; to Barry, diffident and self-conscious, the action was a deliberate attempt to humiliate him, the drawling remark an intentional effort to complete his confusion. A wave of hot anger, searing as the breath of a furnace, swept over him. All the accumulated hatred for this sneering young libertine surged to the surface. Like a whiplash Barry's fist shot out, thudded solidly against flesh, knocked the languid Steve Moley completely out of the chair.

With a pantherlike leap Barry was on him, hands searching swiftly for the gun he knew Steve would attempt to draw. Barbara's sharp command went unheeded. He caught Moley's wrist as the weapon was wrenched from its holster, twisted it sharply, heard the gun strike the veranda floor. Groping fingers found it, tossed it swiftly into the shadows of the porch; then, panting, Barry got to his feet and stood waiting.

Moley got up slowly, and even in the darkness Barry could feel the burning intensity of his gaze. He felt Barbara grasp him by the arm and in the white heat of his anger brushed her roughly aside. With a cry of indignation she thrust herself between them.

"Barry Weston, you ought to be ashamed of yourself! Striking a man who was sitting in a chair and then trying to push me aside! I think you've gone absolutely crazy. Go home and don't come back—ever. I don't want to see you again." Instantly she turned to Moley, her voice softening. "Did he hurt you, Steve?"

Barry stood there for a moment, his cup of bitterness full. Of course he was to blame; that hot temper of his was constantly getting him into trouble. If Barbara only knew Steve Moley as he knew him; but she didn't. Girls didn't hear the gossip of saloon and store; folk diligently kept from them the more sordid and shabby facts of life. Indistinctly he could see her brushing Steve's cheek with her handkerchief, and he experienced a little savage thrill of satisfaction. It would take more than a bit of lace to wipe away the brand he had placed there. Abruptly he turned and strode from the gallery. Flinging himself into the saddle he headed the horse towards town.

At the sound of hoofs, Barbara came to the edge of the gallery and stood looking after him. Her face still burned with resentment, but even then a little voice was whispering that perhaps she had judged too harshly. She tried to stifle it.

Steve moved over beside her, fingers still caressing his sore cheek.

"The yellow pup!" he said. "Knows better than to stand up to me. Had to hit me when I was sittin' down."

"Steve, you shouldn't have tripped him."

"That wasn't what riled him. He's jealous. Right now he's carryin' with him a picture of you and me makin' love in the dark."

She turned on him indignantly. "We weren't making love, Steve Moley, and you know it! Don't you even dare suggest that we were!"

"Sure not. I was just foolin'. Come on; let's sit down again." An arm slipped tentatively about her slim waist, but she twisted away.

"I don't feel like it, Steve. I'm going in. Good night."

She left him abruptly. Steve stood for a few seconds looking at the door which had been shut in his face. He was frowning, and his lips were curled in the sneer which had become characteristic of him. He was older than Barry by two years, and to him Barbara Dawn was a kid; an adorable kid, to be sure, but a kid just the same. Her treatment of him rankled.

"Needs takin' down a peg or two," he mumbled finally, and fashioned a cigarette. When it was going nicely, he strolled from the gallery and with the aid of lighted matches found his gun. Getting on his horse he, too, headed for town.

By the time Barry reached Mescal, the hot flame of anger had simmered to a smouldering blaze which was ready to flare at the slightest suggestion of a draft. He dropped from his horse at the Silver Palace hitch rack, jerked a slipknot in the rein, and entered the saloon. Clement Dawn, Barbara's older brother, stood leaning against the bar. Barry ranged himself alongside his friend and ordered whiskey. Clement eyed him wonderingly, but accepted the drink Barry bought for him.

Barry tossed off his liquor, repressing a shudder as he did so. He did not like the taste of the stuff, but men drank it, and Barry liked to think of himself as a man. Clement spoke a bit anxiously.

"What's the matter, Barry? You're white as a sheet. Sick?"

"Clem, I'm so mad I'm like to bust. I stopped at the house on my way to town. The gallery was dark. When I climbed the steps Barbara called to me, and I thought she was alone in the hammock. She wasn't. Steve Moley was with her."

Clement's face hardened. "Was, huh?"

"Yes. Clem, we know what he is; Barbara doesn't. It burned me up to find him there. You ought to warn her against him. In a nice way, I mean."

"I'll talk to her."

"Don't be rough. She just doesn't understand that it will hurt her to be associated with that scum. You're her brother; you can tell her easy like."

"Sure, I'll tell her. What that Steve Moley needs is a good dose of lead medicine, and he's sure goin' to get it before long. See you later, Barry."

He nodded and walked purposefully away. Barry watched until he had gone, then, feeling a bit reckless, ordered another drink. It left him dizzy, and he went outside to get some air. The sidewalk was deserted. He heard the beat of hoofs and thought at first it was Clement on his way home; but the sounds approached rather than receded, and presently a horseman swung up to the rack and dismounted. As he stepped within range of the Palace lights Barry recognized him. It was Steve Moley.

Steve carelessly draped a rein across the rail and, ducking beneath it, stepped to the walk. Barry was standing by the swinging doors, and at sight of him Steve stopped abruptly.

"I want to talk to you," said Barry.

Moley stared at him, his black eyes glinting. "I don't want no talk out of you. I'm not sittin' down now."

"You're goin' to listen to me, Steve. It won't take long; I can put it in very few words. It's this: keep away from Barbara Dawn."

The sneer on Moley's lips became more pronounced. "You danged meddler—tellin' me what to do! Chew on that and see how you like it!"

He lunged forward, striking viciously. Barry ducked, and the hard fist glanced off the side of his head. His own fist swept upward in an arc and landed squarely on Moley's chin. It was not a knockout punch, but the force of it sent Moley sprawling backward, dazed and dizzy. He brought up against the hitch rail, fell, and rolled into the street. His horse reared, tearing loose the reins, and wheeled away from the rack. Barry's mount was prancing nervously, and in that instant Weston hoped he'd trample Steve into the dust; but Moley rolled clear, got to his knees, and clung to the rack waiting for his brain to clear. In the light which streamed from the saloon Barry could see his face plainly. His eyes were glinting and the thin lips were drawn away from his teeth, giving him the appearance of a snarling wolf.

Quite suddenly he pulled himself to his feet, his hand flashing for the gun at his hip. Barry saw the glint of light on the steel barrel, and his hand streaked for his own weapon. The action was instinctive; never before had he drawn his gun on a man.

The hot rage within him was extinguished as suddenly as though he had been plunged into an icy pool. His head cleared, his muscles steadied. He caught the flash of Moley's gun, felt the hot breath of the slug on his cheek, even heard the sound of lead plunking into the building behind him. Although he had never practiced drawing, the old gun came out of its holster as though it had been greased. He held his elbow close to his side and shot from the hip.

Moley staggered under the impact of the slug, teetered on his heels for a moment, then plunged face down in the dust. And in that one short second Barry became horribly aware of the enormity of the thing he had done.

"My God!" he cried, and ran to Moley's side. He lifted the man in his arms. Moley was limp, and his head lolled as Barry raised him. "Steve!" he cried. "Wake up, man!" But Moley did not respond.

Barry glanced about him. Voices came to him from the inside of the Palace, and he could hear the thud of boots on the wooden floor. In another moment they would come rushing from the place, guns in their hands. He would be caught, and without any defense. He had shot Steve Moley, the son of the town's most influential citizen. Son of Judge Moley, who held the sheriff in the palm of his hand and administered the high justice, the middle, and the low! And he couldn't explain the reason for the quarrel. He'd die before he'd drag Barbara's name into this. They'd hang him higher than Haman.

He dropped the inert body into the dust and sprang for his horse. The animal, nervous, backed to the full length of the rein. Barry jerked it loose, swung the pinto, grasped the horn. Men were streaming from the saloon. Barry yelled at the horse, and as the animal lunged into full stride, ran with him for a few yards, then vaulted into the saddle. Bending low, he headed the pinto for home.

The sweep of the wind on his cheeks helped restore his faculties. He brushed his hand across his forehead and removed it covered with cold sweat. He fought against the emotion which engulfed him, striving to think clearly. There would be no safety for him at the ranch; he must flee the state entirely. But first he would tell his mother. She was a little woman, but she was stanch. She would understand, and she would help.

He flung himself off the gelding outside the house. The livingroom light still burned. As he passed through the doorway he could see her still busy with her mending. She looked up, smiling as usual; then her face sobered at sight of the desperate light in his eyes.

"Barry! What's wrong, son?"

He crossed to her side, dropped on his knees by her chair. "Ma, I've done somethin' awful! Steve Moley— I've shot him!"

"Shot him!" He met her startled gaze with a look of such utter misery that she impulsively drew him to her. "Tell me about it," she said softly.

He did; and somehow as he unburdened himself he began to feel better. When he had finished, he withdrew from her embrace and eyed her anxiously.

"Son, we've been taught that to kill a man is a horrible thing," she said slowly. "But out here where men must kill sometimes in order to live, it doesn't seem so awful. Steve drew on you and fired before you pulled your gun. You shot in self-defense, and if you could prove it any jury would exonerate you. But you can't prove it, and Horace Moley will hound you to the gallows if you stay to fight the charge. So you'll have to run, Barry." She got to her feet in that swift, birdlike way of hers, and started for the kitchen. "You make up a blanket roll. Take extra clothing and plenty of cartridges. I'll fix a package of food and fill a canteen with coffee. If you carry your own supplies you can keep clear of towns."

He followed her impulsively, grasped her by the shoulders and swung her about. "Ma, you're a brick!" he said, and kissed her.

The matter of outfitting did not take long. Fortunately his step-father was in bed. Within fifteen minutes he had strapped a goodly sized package behind the cantle and had tied a filled rifle boot on the saddle. His mother stood on the gallery watching as he mounted the pinto. He rode over to her and, leaning from the saddle, held her to him.

"Good-by, ma," he said brokenly.

"Good-by, son. Ride north. Don't falter and don't waste time blaming yourself. You did the only thing possible, and no matter what others think, God knows the truth. Get word to me where you are. Here—take this money. Be brave and true, and—and be—a good— boy."

She broke down then. Barry kissed her and straightened in the saddle. He could hear her sobbing as he rode away. He sat very stiff and erect, and a lump the size of a melon seemed to have caught in his throat. He bit his lip and dashed an angry hand across his eyes.

Men, he knew, were not supposed to weep.

CHAPTER II

EXILE

BARRY rode north, avoiding the towns, sleeping in out-of-the-way places, leaving the trail at the remotest sign of another traveller. In time he crossed into New Mexico, pushed onward into Colorado, where, safe from pursuit, he worked for a cattle outfit during the fall roundup.

Here it was that he risked sending a letter to his mother, telling her of his escape, and asking that she address him under an assumed name at the town of Pike. When he was sure that sufficient time had elapsed, he went into the combination store and post-office with the intention of inquiring for mail.

A man was seated on the counter dangling his feet. Barry caught his keen look as he stepped up to the window, and at the same moment saw the gleam of a metal star half hidden beneath his coat. Barry had instructed his mother to write him under the name of Butler; now, apprehensive that the officer was waiting to seize the claimant of such a letter, he asked for mail under an entirely different name.

Of course there was none, and Barry turned away.
The heartbreaking part about it was that while the
postmaster was looking through the general delivery
letters, Barry caught sight of one addressed to John
Butler in his mother's handwriting.

He returned to Pike on several occasions after that,
but always the sheriff was in the store; and he finally
gave up his efforts to secure the letter. Had he but
known it, the officer had never heard of either Barry
Weston or John Butler. He was a brother of the store-
keeper and boarded with him.

At the end of the roundup, Barry headed north
again, holding to the trail until he reached Sheridan,
Wyoming. Having saved his money, he stayed awhile
at this town, hearing finally of an outfit across the line
in Montana that needed men. He applied for a job,
and got it.

He did not write again. Walt Bascomb, postmaster
at Mescal, owed his job to the influence of Horace
Moley. One letter from Barry had already passed
through his hands; the next one might be intercepted.
In an effort to forget his Texas home and the ones
he loved, Barry plunged into the work of the range
with a dogged determination that won him swift
advancement.

Spring came, and with it calving time. Barry had
toughened and hardened under the rigors of a severe
winter. The determination to win a place for himself
in this north country had left its stamp upon him.
He had become more serious of mein and feature; his
blue eyes were somber; he rarely smiled.

There was no regret for the shooting of Steve Moley. He knew that if he had given Steve the chance to fire another shot, he would have been killed. But he realized now that his hot temper might easily lead him into a quarrel that was not entirely justified, and he rigorously fought that hot emotion which arose within him and prompted him to act before he had thought.

As a result he became somewhat slow of speech, forcing himself to turn things over in his mind before delivering an opinion. When angered, he formed the habit of staring fixedly at the object of his ire for a short space of time. Thus he was able to control his passion; but once decided that retaliation was justified, he went into action with the speed and fury of a cougar.

By degrees he shed his exaggerated ideas of what constituted a man. He no longer swaggered, and he drank infrequently and sparingly. His curly hair was still a source of despair; but now that there was no Barbara Dawn in his life, he didn't take the pains to control it, but conceded to Nature a victory that she would have won in any event.

Always his mind was busy with thoughts of his mother and Barbara and Clement. They seemed with him constantly in spirit, and at times he longed so desperately for a sight of them that he would mount his horse and ride swiftly across the rolling rangeland in an effort to lose the urge in the sweep of the wind. Barbara had sent him home. She said she never wanted to see him again. He realized with a feeling of despair that perhaps she never would.

He had long since sold the pinto. The animal was too conspicuous, and he had learned that a horse of solid color was more dependable and seemed to possess more stamina.

Fall came, and then winter with its constant worries about drift fence and starving cattle. Spring and calf roundup, summer range, fall again—one season followed another swiftly. Always he worked. In his third year he was made foreman of Hank Steven's big spread. His responsibilities doubled, and he had less time to think of Texas. He learned to handle men, to judge them, to reward and punish. Once they were bothered by rustlers, and Barry led a party of cattlemen against them. They were trapped and exterminated. Barry was forced to kill two of them, and in one case his habit of thinking before acting nearly cost him his life. When he was recovering from the wound he had received it occurred to him that, as in the case of Steve Moley, the emergency had found him calm, almost cold.

Spring of the fifth year of exile found him a man of twenty-four, tall, broad of shoulder, somber of countenance, but entirely master of himself. The twentieth of May was his birthday. It dawned cold and dismal with the threat of rain in the air. He felt suddenly depressed, and in an effort to escape the drab dreariness he rode to Sheridan. At a saloon he had a drink which strangled without warming. He ordered another. For once in his life he felt like getting soddenly drunk. On the verge of tossing it off he stopped. A man had stepped to a place at the bar beside him. His clothes were ragged, his face unshaven, his gray hair straggled about his shoulders; but there was something in his makeup that Barry recognized. He looked into the back-bar mirror and studied the man's face until he was sure of the identification.

"Howdy, George," he said quietly.

The man turned an apathetic face towards him, then the old eyes brightened and the seamed face crinkled in a smile.

"Barry Weston, by the eternal!"

"George Brent, of Mescal, Texas!" They shook hands delightedly. "George, what under the sun brings you up here?"

"I'm ridin' the grub line, Barry," said George sadly. "Funny, ain't it? When you left I was runnin' my own spread, the old Slash B. Now it's gone, and I'm plumb busted and just about down and out."

He turned to the liquor which he had ordered. Barry left his own drink untouched.

"This is my birthday, and we're goin' to celebrate," Barry told him. "We'll hunt up a restaurant and have the best meal they can turn out. Come along."

"I—I ain't got much *dinero,* Barry," apologized Brent. "And I ain't a bit hungry. You eat and I'll watch."

"You'll eat with me, old-timer, and you'll talk. Gosh, George, I'm full of questions. First off, how's mother?"

"Now don't you start askin' questions now. Wait till we git to the rest'rant and I'll give you the whole story while we're eatin'. Lots of things have happened in Mescal Basin since you left."

No more was said until they were seated in a cafe with a generous meal spread before them. Brent plunged into his story without any urging on Barry's part.

"You asked me how I got up here, and I reckon I'd better tell you that first. It ain't a long story. Mescal Basin is on the down grade—been goin' down steadily for a couple of years. Two seasons of drouth and cattle disease danged near wrecked us, Matt Billings especially. Yeah, your ma's Flyin' W and the Cinchbuckle was hit too, but not as hard as Matt's MB. The sickness started on his range, but luckily for the rest of us it was fenced—only spread in the Basin that is—and the rest of us managed to save somethin'.

"About a year ago I'd reached the end of the string. As a last resort I went to Judge Moley to see could I get me a loan of some money. You know folks always figgered he was rich. I didn't have much hope— jest took a reckless plunge, you might say. Well, Horace agreed to lend me ten thousand dollars to re-stock, takin' a mortgage on the Slash B as collateral for the loan. I give him the mortgage right willin', for I had everything to gain and nothin' but a few scrawny cows and a dry range to lose. I bought me some prime breedin' stock and started out to build up the old Slash B. Well, sir, I'd hardly turned my new herd into pasture before the whole danged outfit was rustled."

"Rustled!"

"Yes, sir. Never had no rustlin' of any account in the Basin before, but they sure stripped me clean. Me and the boys started out after 'em, but they split the herd into small bunches and hazed 'em through the south hills and across the Border. Leastwise, that's what we think they did; never could find out for sure. Since then some of the others have lost stock—the Cinchbuckle and the Flyin' W. Seems like an outlaw named Tug Groody has a gang operatin' in the south hills, and it ain't far from there to the Border."

"What's the matter with the sheriff?"

"The same thing that's ailed him all along—laziness and inefficiency. Yeah, Sam Hodge still has the job. Horace Moley gits him reelected every term some way or other. Well, Sam chased around in the hills lookin' for Tug, but somehow he never caught up with him. As I said, they cleaned me complete. When the time came to make a payment on my note, I went to Horace and asked for an extension. A bank had opened up in Mescal run by a feller named Alonzo J. Frothingham, and Horace told me he had discounted my note and turned the mortgage over to the bank. I went to Frothington, but he refused to give me any additional time and sold me out. The Slash B was bought by Steve Moley."

Barry stiffened in his chair. "Steve Moley!"

"Yeah. What's the matter?"

Barry had gone white. "Steve Moley! I—I thought—"

"You'd killed him? Shucks, no. I wish you had. Didn't nobody write you? He got well and is onerier than ever. If ever a jasper needed some killin' it's Steve; but your bullet didn't do the trick—worse luck."

Barry drew a deep breath. "Then I didn't kill him! I can go back!"

"Sure you can. But there's mighty little left to go back to, except your mother."

"Tell me about her, George. She's well?"

Brent lowered his head and for a moment was busy trying to corral some peas on his knife. Barry leaned over the table and gripped him by an arm.

"George, why don't you answer? She's well, isn't she?"

Brent looked up soberly. "Well—no, Barry, she ain't. She had a shock a year or so ago. When I left she was in bed, but she was gettin' better. Only—well, them things come back, you know; and now that it's safe, I reckon you'd better be gittin' back there to look after her."

"How long has it been since you saw her?"

"Barry, I reckon it's close to a year. But don't take it so hard, son. I'm sure she's all right. Maybe I gave you the wrong hunch when I said you ought to go back. I just meant that the Flyin' W needs you now that your step-father has gone haywire."

Barry frowned. "What do you mean?"

"Chet Lewis is a bum," said Brent deliberately. "I know you never liked him, but I'd be bound to say the same thing if you did. Right after you left he took to drinkin' and loafin'. The ranch run down somethin' terrible. Lately he's been pesterin' your ma to sell out to the Moleys. Horace and Steve must be gittin' land crazy. I heard they were after Barbara Dawn to sell the Cinchbuckle too."

"Let me get this straight, George. You say they're after Barbara to sell the Cinchbuckle. What's the matter with her father and Clement? They used to run that spread."

"Charley Dawn died a couple years ago. He left the ranch to Barbara and Clement and Clay. And now that Clement's gone—but maybe you didn't hear about that either?"

"George, you're the first man to bring me news from Mescal in the past five years."

"Well, Clement and Steve had a run-in. Steve kept hangin' around the Cinchbuckle, mostly when Clement was away. Heard tell that Clem had ordered him off the spread. One day he walked in on 'em when Steve was badgerin' her to sell. They had words, and Clement popped him."

"George, he didn't!"

"I'll tell a man he did. Knocked Steve plumb loose from his boot heels. The very next night Clem tangled with Cal Garth, one of Steve's pet gunmen. It was back of the Palace and nobody saw it. There were two shots, and when the crowd run out Cal was layin' on the ground deader'n a mackerel. Ace Polmateer, who owns the Palace, and his two bouncers were first on the spot. They kept the crowd away until Sheriff Hodge got there. At the inquest Hodge swore that Cal's gun was fully loaded and in his holster. That made it murder, and if Clem ever comes back to Mescal he'll sure swing for it."

"Clement never shot a man without giving him a chance," said Barry flatly.

Brent shrugged. "There are lots of folks that believe the same, me included; but when the other jigger is found with his gun unfired and in his holster, especially a gunman like Garth, there ain't but one verdict a jury can bring in."

"So Clement had to run for it," said Barry slowly.

"Yeah. That left the Cinchbuckle in the hands of Barbara and Clay, her younger brother. The girl runs it, and, Barry, she is one little lady to tie to! Knows her cows. And han'some? Son, she's as purty as a new yaller buggy with red wheels."

George finished his meal with a sigh of satisfaction. Barry had pushed back his plate when he heard the news of his mother's illness. Now he got to his feet. "George, I'm headin' back to Mescal. What are you aimin' to do?"

"Look for a job like I been doin', I reckon. It sure is tough. I look like a bum and feel like one. And I'm gittin' old."

"We'll fix that in a hurry," said Barry tersely. "I've got a boss that ranks Ace high, and I'm takin' you to see him. Come along."

They went to a store where, despite Brent's protests, Barry bought him some new clothes. When a barber had clipped his hair and shaved him, George Brent was a new man in appearance.

"I'm thankin' you, Barry," he said quietly. "If you aim to give me a job I'll pay you back out of my first month's wages."

Soberly they rode from Sheridan, Barry's joy at the reunion dampened by the news which Brent had been forced to impart. Presently he began to ask questions, and Brent answered brightly in an effort to divert. Yes, his mother often spoke of him. True blue, Mrs. Lewis. Chet couldn't talk her into selling the Flying W; she felt that it belonged to Barry even if the title was in her name. Ace Polmateer had added a dance floor to the Palace and had engaged a string of girls. Steve Moley was crazy about one of them. No, he didn't mess around Barbara much; she was keeping company off and on with Alonzo J. Frothingham, the president of the new bank. And so on until Barry's range captured their attention.

They dismounted at headquarters, and Barry led his friend directly to Hank Stevens. The introduction was short and to the point.

"Boss, meet up with a friend from Texas. Name's George Brent, and he sure savvies cows. He's your new foreman."

"You're not leavin' Barry?"

"Yes. Brent tells me that my mother is—very sick. Maybe she is already gone. I got to go back to her, Hank."

Stevens had Barry's full confidence. "How about that shootin' scrape?"

"The man didn't die after all. If he's had a hand in mother's illness—if he worried her until she broke down, I may have to finish the job. Anyhow, I got to go back. Boss, we have some good men on the spread, but they're all cowboys. Brent is a rancher; he owned his own spread in Texas. He'll make you a good fore-man."

Hank was a man of quick decisions. "Your recom-mend is good enough for me, Barry. Brent, you're on the payroll as foreman startin' today."

Barry spoke tersely. "You can draw up a check for the money you've been holdin' for me. I'll cash it at Sheridan on my way south. While you're doin' it I'll be gettin' my outfit together." He nodded shortly and left the room.

The two men looked after him speculatively.

"There goes a square, upstandin' man if there ever was one," said Hank. "I sure hate to lose him."

George Brent nodded his agreement. "He's changed a heap. Back in Mescal Basin folks remember him as a wild young kid. I got a hunch that somebody's goin' to be su'prized; mighty dawggoned su'prized."

CHAPTER III

MURDER ON THE TRAIL

BARRY WESTON reined in his horse and sat the saddle listening. The sound of three distinct shots had been borne to him on the afternoon breeze, the first two in quick succession, the other after a short interval. Had the shots been equally spaced he would have taken them for the help signal in general use; but as it was they might mean anything from harmless target shooting to a battle for life. After a moment he urged his horse onward at a slow lope.

He sniffed the air eagerly, gazed about him at every familiar landmark. Night should find him at the side of his mother. His pleasant anticipation was tinged with a shade of apprehension. Suppose he were too late? The thought caused him to spur his mount, only to rein in almost instantly. The horse had served him faithfully; for a full month he had carried Barry steadily towards home, always willing, never faltering. Now within hours of his destination, there was no necessity to hurry him.

The country was rolling and rocky, with occasional

patches of scrub timber and thorny chaparral. Presently the horse topped a rise, and Barry drew rein quickly and backed the animal to an outcropping of rock over which he could peer.

Before him the stage road dipped gently into a stone-studded hollow, to rise again on the far side to the crest of still another ridge. Down this latter slope a horseman was rushing, bent low over the neck of his mount. Almost at once a compact group of pursuers topped the rise, quirts rising and falling, sun glinting on their weapons. Even as Barry watched, the horseman in the lead turned in his saddle and fired rapidly with a six-gun.

Barry remained behind his rock shelter. Thus far there was no call for interference. The pursued might be a criminal; the pursuers, a posse.

The horseman in the lead crossed the flat bottom of the depression and put his horse to the slope which led to Barry's hiding place. Weston could see the fellow's eyes now. They were staring wildly, desperately. He was leaning as far over as his saddle horn would permit.

The climb slowed his horse's speed, and the pursuers perceptibly closed the gap between them and their quarry. Now, as they reached the foot of the slope, their leader pulled his mount to a stop, raised his six-gun, and, taking deliberate aim, fired. The fleeing man jerked erect in his saddle, swayed, tossed about for a few jumps like a sack of straw in a bouncing wagon, then slipped from the saddle, rolled, and lay still.

Barry drew the carbine from its sheath under his

leg and rode out to the top of the rise. At this range he was out of reach of their six-guns, while his rifle easily commanded them. He fired a warning shot, then rode slowly down the trail towards the prostrate man.

The pursuers drew up sharply, their horses restive. For a moment they conversed, then suddenly spurred their mounts in a charge straight up the slope. Barry fired again, and one of the horses plunged forward to the earth, throwing its rider heavily. Another shot and a horseman pulled up, his left arm dangling. Swerving their mounts from the trail, they circled, heading for the foot of the declivity.

The man who had been unseated got to his feet and started running in a zig-zag course down the grade. When he reached his waiting companions, one of them extended a hand and drew him to the horse's back; then the whole six rode swiftly up the opposite slope and disappeared over the ridge.

Barry dismounted by the prostrate man and rolled him over on his back. The fellow was short and stocky, with that appearance of untidiness which clings to some persons despite their efforts to escape it. He was shot through and through, and could not possibly live very long. Barry got his canteen and forced some of the water into the man's mouth. There was little else he could do. He was on the open road, several hours' ride from Mescal, and moving the man was out of the question. He squatted on his heels and smoked thoughtfully, shielding the fellow from the rays of the sun with his body.

He heard a coughing gasp and looked down at the

wounded man. His eyes were open and he was trying to speak. Barry quickly raised his head, wiped the froth from his lips, and gave him a drink of water.

"Thanks," gasped the man feebly, and lay back, panting. His lips moved again, and Barry had to put his head close to them in order to hear.

"I'm—done for—ain't I?"

"You're pretty hard hit, pardner."

There was a short interval of silence, broken by a coughing spell which brought on a hemorrhage.

"Better not try to talk," advised Barry.

The man clamped his white lips together and gazed wildly up at Barry. He gasped the words with a distinct effort. "Damned—double-crosser! Oughta knowed —he'd do it." He uttered a bitter laugh which brought on a coughing spell. Barry raised his head until the paroxysm had passed. As he was lowering him, the man spoke again, faintly, haltingly. "Buy—steal— kill!" He closed his eyes, his strength entirely gone.

Barry leaned over him and spoke sharply. "Listen, pardner; who are you talkin' about? Who shot you, and why?"

The eyelids fluttered open, the lips moved weakly. No audible sound escaped them, although Barry placed his ear close and strained to hear. In his impatience he shook the man gently in an effort to rouse him. "His name?" he kept repeating. "Tell me his name?" But the man had gone lax in his arms and at last Barry realized that he was dead.

Carefully he examined the contents of the man's pockets in an effort to identify him. There were a few trinkets, some change, and a wallet the contents of which caused Barry to exclaim in amazement. He thumbed through the thick wad of banknotes. Five thousand dollars! No wonder the fellow had been waylaid.

Barry put the wallet into an inside pocket for safe keeping, then caught up the man's horse and roped the limp body over the saddle. Using the rein as a lead rope, he continued on his way.

"Buy—steal—kill." What had the fellow meant by that? Steal and kill were easily understandable; but why the buy? George Brent's story of how the Moleys were attempting to buy the Cinchbuckle and the Flying W had, of course, impressed him; but surely there could be no connection here. There was the possibility, though, that the man's pursuers might be the rustler gang George had mentioned. Although the distance had been too great for positive identification, Barry had seen that the leader—he who had shot this man—was big and broad and bewhiskered. Barry believed he would know him if he were to meet him again. And certainly one of the others would carry his arm in a sling for some time to come.

The sun was low when he rode into Mescal. Barry found himself gazing about him much like a colt returning to the home pasture. Same false-fronted buildings, a bit more warped and faded from the five years' sun and rain; the Silver Palace of Ace Polmateer, easily the largest establishment in town and shining with a coat of fresh paint; Bascomb's store, also renovated; a new brick building bearing the legend CAT-

TLEMAN'S BANK; the squat, drab office of Horace
Moley, attorney-at-law and justice of the peace. Livery
barn and corral, feed store and harness shop. All unchanged. Even the streets wore the same old ruts which
crossed and criss-crossed like the wrinkles in the face
of a very tired old man. But it all spelled home.

The people on the main street stared curiously, a few
of them following along the sidewalks. Some of them
Barry knew, but none recognized him in the dusk. He
rode straight to a building labeled SHERIFF'S
OFFICE and drew rein before it. Sam Hodge stood
in the doorway, picking his teeth. He caught sight of
Barry and the laden horse, and walked to the hitch
rack.

"What you got there?" he asked, and looked up at
Barry.

"Know me, Sam?"

The sheriff squinted hard, then jerked erect and
backed away a step.

"Barry Weston! Who in hell you shot now?"

Barry stared at him, habit suppressing the hot words
which rose to his lips. Presently he spoke, explaining.
Hodge walked into the street and callously raised the
dangling head of the dead man.

"Huh!" he grunted, allowing it to fall again. "It's
that Slater jigger that's been hangin' around the Cinchbuckle. Find anything on him?"

"This," said Barry, and handed him the wallet.

The sheriff counted the contents, his eyes widening
in surprise. "All that *dinero!* And everybody thought

he was a bum. Huh! I'll put this in my safe until we can locate his folks."

A question came from somebody in the crowd. "And what are you going to do about the killer? It is evident, isn't it? that Tug Groody did this."

Barry turned quickly to look at the speaker. He saw a tall, rather gaunt man, with a long, wolfish face and a mane of iron-gray hair. He was wearing a shabby black frock coat, baggy black trousers, and a motheaten beaver hat. Horace Moley, big man of Mescal, had also changed but little.

"Why, I'll git a posse together first thing in the mornin'. Ain't no use ridin' now; we sure can't trail in the dark." Hodge turned back to the office with the wallet.

"I think it would be wise to copy the numbers on those banknotes," said Moley. "This man may have stolen them for all we know." He entered the office on the heels of the sheriff and closed the door behind him. Presently they emerged, talking.

"I'll check up on these numbers," said Moley. "In the meantime, try to get in touch with the man's relatives." He nodded shortly to Hodge and walked across the sidewalk to where Barry sat his horse. For a moment Moley stood looking up into Barry's face, his own features inscrutable.

"So you've come back, eh?"

"Yes."

"Aiming to stay?"

"Why, I reckon so."

"Well, I can't say that you're welcome; our memory of you isn't a pleasing one."

"I have a few unpleasant recollections myself."

For a brief moment the two men exchanged level, appraising glances; then Moley turned abruptly away and started across the street towards his office.

Sam Hodge came to the edge of the sidewalk and spoke gruffly. "All right, Weston, you can go. I'll take charge of Slater's horse."

Barry wheeled away from the rack. No longer could he curb his impatience to reach the Flying W. He wanted to ask Hodge about his mother, but the sheriff's attitude had killed all desire to question him. He tried to ease his mind by concentrating on the murder of Slater. Sam Hodge had said the man had been hanging around the Cinchbuckle. The Moleys were trying to buy that spread, and Slater had died with the word "buy" on his lips. George had also said that the Cinchbuckle had been losing stock, and had blamed the loss on a gang of rustlers led by Tug Groody. And it was undoubtedly Tug Groody's men who had murdered Slater. There *was* a connection there, but so vague a one that Barry was unable to trace it to any reasonable conclusion.

He could never explain why he slowed to a walk when he neared the ranch house. Perhaps it was the natural dread of finding his worst fears realized that caused him to check his horse. Even when he rounded the east wing and saw the light in his mother's bedroom he held to this slow pace. On the soft turf the sound of hoofs was almost inaudible. Then he saw a horse at the hitch rack, and on an impulse rode to a corner of the gallery and tied there.

Noiselessly he stepped to the gallery. There was a light in the living room, and peering through a window he could see two men leaning over the desk in one corner. He recognized one of them as his step-father, Chet Lewis; the other, although his back was turned, he knew to be Steve Moley.

Gently he raised the latch and pulled. The door was barred. Barry considered for a moment, then moved silently from the gallery and circled the house. The rear door was unfastened. He stooped and unbuckled his spurs, placing them in his chaps pocket; then entered and closed the door behind him.

He was in the kitchen. Before him was the dining room, and beyond that the lighted living room. There was sufficient illumination to permit him to avoid the furniture as he made his way softly to the living room entrance. There he stopped, watching and listening.

His step-father was seated at the desk, a pen gripped in his hand, laboriously writing. Before him were spread a number of papers. Steve Moley looked over his shoulder. As Barry watched, the older man jerked back in his chair and spoke testily.

"I can't do it, Steve. My hand shakes so's I can't even stay on the line."

"Go on and write," grated Moley. "What difference does it make if the signature is shaky? She's sick and weak; it'll look all the more natural."

Barry felt the hot blood mounting to his head, and only the force of stern habit restrained him from springing at the conspirators. They were forging his mother's name to some document. But she still lived; Moley's words assured him of that. Perhaps it was this knowledge which helped him keep a grip on himself and remain, muscles tense and blood pounding, to see the thing through.

Moley went on: "Go ahead; practice some more. And for gosh sake, relax. You're grippin' that pen like a drownin' man hangin' onto an oar. Loosen up."

"Steve, if Barry ever finds this out he'll kill me!"

"You poor weaklin', quit your belly-achin'. Barry ain't findin' nothin' out. He won't be back until it's too late to do a thing about it. Now get busy and sign that deed. You can witness it in your own handwritin', and I'll be the other witness. Go ahead; sign it."

Again Chet Lewis bent to his task; Barry heard the scratch of the pen as he wrote, swiftly, desperately. Flinging the pen on the desk he leaned back in his chair and swore. "There it is. It's the best I can do."

Moley seized the deed and held it up exultantly. "It's perfect! Chet, all you needed was somebody to prod you. The old lady'd have to acknowledge that signature herself!"

"Think so?" came a cold voice from the doorway.

Both men wheeled, Moley's hand moving instinctively towards his gun. The paper to which he clung hampered him, and before he could draw the weapon Barry was speaking.

"Don't do it, Steve. I aim to make sure the next time I shoot."

His step-father had twisted about in his chair and

was staring with wild, red-rimmed eyes and slack jaw. His face was a pasty white. Moley was trembling with rage and frustration; only the certain knowledge that this man would kill him prevented his forcing the issue.

Barry stepped into the room, his stride springy like that of a stalking cougar. Even to Moley's rage-heated brain seeped the knowledge that this man was infinitely more dangerous than the boy who had outshot him five years before. Weston had filled out, hardened; his face had lost its youthful curves; the jaw muscles were rigid and inflexible. There was a certain definite something which stamped him as capable, dominant, entirely sure of himself.

"I'll take the deed, Steve." Barry paid not the slightest attention to the cowed Lewis.

Under the spell of that compelling gaze, Moley involuntarily stretched out the hand which clutched the paper. Barry briefly glanced at the document, then tore it to shreds.

"We won't bother with the law, it's too slow, and I can scotch my own snakes. Get out, Steve; and don't ever set foot on the Flyin' W again. Start movin'."

Red rage suddenly blinded Steve Moley. Who was this upstart to order him about? What right had he to come back and interfere with the plans of himself and his father? With a wild oath he snatched at his gun, and this time there was no paper to hamper him.

Barry had been praying that he would make such a move. Sternly he had held himself in; now all the accumulated fury within him surged to the surface. As though hurled from a catapult he sprang at Moley.

His tense fingers gripped the wrist of Steve's gun hand, wrenched it so violently that Moley screamed with pain. The gun flew from his hand to clatter on the floor a dozen feet away.

Moley lashed out with his free fist only to have his arm seized in an iron grip and forced down in front of him. With his left hand, Barry pinioned both the fellow's wrists, and with the palm of his right slapped him again and again on the cheek. They were vicious, stinging blows; but the ignominy of them cut far deeper than the ringing slaps.

Whirling the livid Moley, Barry propelled him to the doorway, drew the bolt, and pushed him through the entrance to the gallery.

"Get on your horse and ride," he said thickly, and stood there to make sure that his order was obeyed.

Steve, shaking with rage and humiliation, leaped on his horse, wheeled the animal from the rack, then turned and spat out every vile epithet that crowded to his tongue. Not until Barry made a motion toward his gun did the fellow jerk his horse about and spur him unmercifully from the yard.

Barry went inside to find his step-father cringing in a chair, his eyes wide with apprehension.

"It was a joke, Barry," he wailed. "We was just funnin'—me and Steve. We wasn't goin' to use—"

"Shut up. Chet Lewis, you're a liar by the clock. Quit shakin'; I'm not goin' to hurt you. God knows you deserve killin', but for some reason ma saw fit to marry you, and you're still her husband. Now listen to me. Tomorrow you turn out with the crew—if there are any left—and get to work. You'll eat in the bunk-house and sleep there too. And if you take one drink of liquor and I find it out, I'll use a quirt on you. . . . How's mother?"

"Porely, Barry; porely. She had a shock about a year ago, and she ain't never got over it right. I'm awful worried about her."

Barry flung him a withering look and turned on his heel. In the corridor which led to the east wing, he halted to compose himself, then walked quietly to her door, rapped lightly, and opened it.

She was seated in a rocking chair with a quilt about her shoulders. Her head rested on the back of the chair, and her eyes were closed. How pale and wan she was; how thin and wasted! And her hair had turned completely white. So still was she that for a moment Barry thought that life had fled.

"Ma!" he cried, all the pity and yearning of those five long years surging over him.

Her eyes fluttered open, and such a wonderful change came over her face that he was startled.

"Why—Barry! I was dreaming of you!"

In an instant he was kneeling by her side, holding her frail body close, kissing the soft white hair.

"Ma—dear old ma! It's so good to be back!"

CHAPTER IV

A WEAKLING WITH A WAD

PRESENTLY Barry gently held her from him, surveyed her with a mock frown of sternness. "Now, young lady, another doctor is takin' over your case. Dr. Barry Q. Weston, the Q standin' for quick recovery. We're goin' to have you up and about in no time; a bed room is no place for a lady of your tender years. Now lean back and relax while Dr. Weston gets a chair. Here; let me wrap that quilt about you."

He tucked the cover beneath her shoulders and quickly drew up a chair.

"Speak on, lady, and let the doctor have—what do you call it? the medical history."

Her cheeks were wet, but Barry noticed that a little color had crept into them, and she was smiling.

"Land sakes, I do believe I'm going to like my new doctor."

"Hm-m-m. Well, confidence is half the cure. Speak on, lady."

Haltingly she told him. Immediately after his flight things began to go bad. Although she tried to shield him, Barry gathered that the fault lay with his step-father. Lewis began to neglect the ranch, to drink, and to remain away for days at a stretch. His mother was unable to run the spread and take care of the many household duties at the same time. She had a break-down which sent her to bed for a long while. About a year before his return, Chet Lewis began urging her to sell; but the ranch had been built up by the efforts of Barry's father, and she steadfastly refused to let it go.

"Horace Moley came out to see me, but I stood firm against selling. Chet didn't like it a bit. We began to lose stock, breeders mostly. I hired more men and kept them riding the north line, but it didn't do any good; stock kept disappearing in bunches so small that you'd hardly notice it. With the worry and—and every-thing, I got worse; and one day I just tumbled over. I woke up in bed with my left side paralyzed. But I'm getting better. I can move around a bit if I do it slow; and now that you're back—"

"Of course," said Barry quickly. Not for the world would he let her see how disturbed he was. "A very simple case, lady. I can foresee a complete and rapid recovery. You need fresh air, sunshine, and mild exer-cise. Tomorrow you and the doctor are goin' to take a little walk in the sun, and afterwards you're goin' to be moved to the gallery in the softest rockin' chair I can rig up. Right now the doctor will so far forget his dignity as to make the bed."

He got up and walked over to the four-poster. His mother turned her head to watch him anxiously.

"It's in terrible shape, Barry. Seems like I ain't got the strength to make it right. And the feather mattress and pillows need airing."

"So I see." Barry went to a spare room and stripped the bed of its accessories. He was angry clear through. His step-father could at least have tried to make her comfortable.

Swiftly he changed mattresses and pillows, found fresh sheets and covers.

"There! Fit for a queen, even if it was made up by an amateur. Come; I'll help you."

She was smiling happily as he tenderly tucked her in. "It feels—so good," she whispered; then, "Oh, Barry!"

"Now, now! No cryin'! That ain't part of the cure a-tall. Kiss me goodnight and go to sleep. Remember, you have a walk scheduled for tomorrow."

When he returned to the living room Chet Lewis had gone. It was just as well that he was out of Barry's reach. Barry prowled about the ranch house, finding everywhere dust and dirt and disorder. Lewis had not washed the dishes for several meals.

Barry found some food and prepared it, adding his used dishes to the stack standing in the sink. "Let the lazy bum do them too," he said savagely, and went out to care for his horse. There was a light in the bunk-house, but he did not go near the place. His step-father would be there, and Barry had no desire to encounter him now.

He found his own room just as he had left it, and knew that his mother had kept it ready against his return. The bed was neatly made up, and the covers thrown back for airing. He opened the windows and turned in.

It was some time before he slept. He had left Mescal Basin a placid community where the days slipped peacefully by in the even routine of breeding and raising and selling cattle. He had returned on the heels of a murder to find its people uneasy and harassed and disturbed. Drought and disease had weakened their herds, rustling had further depleted them. The Slash B had been closed out by the bank, and the Moleys had gone land crazy.

It was about the latter that he puzzled most. Why were Horace and his son so anxious to acquire the Flying W and the Cinchbuckle? Horace Moley was no cattleman, and Steve would have his hands full with the Slash B; yet the latter had descended to forgery to gain control of the ranch Barry's mother would not sell. Where did Slater fit in? What was a saddle bum doing with five thousand dollars? The whole thing was a riddle which would require time to solve.

Early in the morning he arose and went out to care for his horse. Chet Lewis and two men had just come from the bunkhouse.

"Is this all the crew?" asked Barry.

"Yeah, Barry, it is. Lately we ain't done so well; things—"

"Things are goin' to be a heap different from now on. You got your orders, boys?"

"Chet says to work on the north fence," drawled one of them.

"Good enough. Hop to it. From now on I'm runnin'

the spread and signin' the pay checks. Lewis, you come with me."

The man reluctantly followed him into the house, and stood in the kitchen looking helplessly about him.

"You can start right here," Barry told him. "Pump some water and use lots of soap. The mop's there in the corner. When you get the place clean—and I mean clean—you can wash up the dishes. Then you tackle the rest of the house."

Lewis protested. "Looky here, Barry, you ain't got no right to make me do things like that. I ain't no hired girl."

"You're sure goin' to give a good imitation of one until this place is clean. Lewis, I got enough against you to wring your neck and win a vote of thanks from the community. You get busy rustlin' that mop. When I get back you'd better have this kitchen straightened out."

While Lewis sullenly pumped water, Barry prepared breakfast for his mother. When he carried it to her room, he found her trying to make the bed.

"Ma!" he said reproachfully, and placed the tray on a chair.

"But I can do it, Barry. I feel lots better."

"No bed makin'. Doctor's orders. Now sit down here and eat your breakfast; then dress in somethin' not too hard to get into, and if you need help, holler."

Half an hour later he assisted her from her room. Walking very slowly, supporting her frail body, he led her to the big gallery and into the sunshine. Slowly they made a circuit of the house, stopping occasionally to look at some feeble shrub or flower which, even though neglected, strove to thrive and blossom.

"See, ma?" he said. "Just like you. A little care and they'll be liftin' their faces to the sun as good as ever."

He filled a big rocker with cushions and saw her comfortably installed in it. When he left her she was smiling and her eyes were very bright.

The kitchen was clean. Not as spotless as his mother had kept it, but quite a creditable job, considering who had done it. He sent Lewis into the living room with broom and dust pan. "I'm goin' to look over the range," he told his step-father. "Mother is out on the gallery. Fella, you'd better treat her right polite, and if she calls for anything, you hop. Savvy?"

Lewis nodded surlily, and Barry went for his horse. All morning he rode over the Flying W, noting sadly the effect of indifference and neglect. Even the appallingly few cattle remaining seemed apathetic and thin. At noon he returned to the ranch house to prepare his mother's dinner and move her chair to a better location. She seemed quite bright and cheerful.

"Chet's cleanin' house," she confided in an awestruck whisper. "Barry, what's come over him?"

"He's atonin' for his sins likely. But don't get all stirred up, ma; he'll be backslidin' before long I reckon."

That afternoon he rode to the north boundary and found the two cowboys listlessly working on the fence which had been built in an effort to keep down rustling. He questioned them closely, deciding that they were worthless and under the domination of Chet Lewis.

They could not—or would not—shed any light on the rustling problem, and Barry left them with the determination to get rid of them as soon as he could find others to replace them.

Pride kept him from the Cinchbuckle. Time had not changed his feelings towards Barbara Dawn, but on that eventful evening five years before she had ordered him off the spread, saying that she did not want to see him again. By this time she had probably relented; but Barry felt that she herself must remove the ban before he could feel free to set foot on the Cinchbuckle again.

When he helped his mother to her room that evening, he noticed with satisfaction the distinct signs of improvement in her condition. Cooped up in that east bed room, she had received the benefit of the sun for only a short period each day; to have remained there much longer must surely have killed her.

"I've got to ride to Mescal for supplies," he told her. "We're short in everything. You mind my leavin' you alone?"

"Land sakes, no, Barry. You run right along. I'm sort of used to being alone. And you—"

"Yes'm," he grinned. "I'll be a good boy."

He rode directly to Bascomb's store, ordered what he wanted, and asked that it be sent out to the ranch the next morning; then, having some time on his hands, walked down to the Silver Palace and entered the saloon.

For a moment he stood looking curiously about him. He hardly knew the place. It was well lighted and roomy, with a fifty-foot bar along the west wall. Down the middle of the room was a double row of tables, and paralleling the east wall were the games. At the far end of the place a platform had been built for dancing and for the show put on by Ace Polmateer's girls. Beyond that he caught sight of a door which evidently led to a small room for private parties.

Leaning indolently against one end of the bar was Ace Polmateer, dark of hair and eye, with the well-groomed mustache and the white, delicate hands of the professional gambler. Seeming to sense Barry's gaze, he turned his head to stare. His expression did not change, but his cool nod told Barry he had been recognized. Weston stepped to the bar and ordered a glass of beer. When he had finished drinking it, he found Polmateer beside him.

"Fill it up again, Joe," Ace ordered the bartender. "I'll take a short one. . . . Well, Barry, back again, eh?"

"Yes." Barry had never liked Polmateer overmuch.

"Staying long?"

"Depends. I see you've fixed up the Palace. That back bar mirror must have cost a small fortune. Sure must be bullet-proof."

"Practically." Polmateer jerked his head towards two men who sat at a table near the end of the bar. They were hard-visaged, keen-eyed characters with gunmen stamped all over them. "Bouncers; only they do their bouncing with lead. No promiscuous shooting inside the Palace, Weston."

"I see. What are the lives of a few drunken punchers beside that mirror, eh?"

"That's the idea. This is a well conducted place. The games are on the square and there is no rough-house. Remember that, Weston."

"Meanin' what?"

Ace shrugged. "You left town after a shooting scrape. Before that you had the reputation of being a buck-wild young hombre. I'm not saying you were at fault in that fight with Steve Moley, but he swears you shot him when he stepped into the light and before he had even drawn his gun."

"That's a lie!"

Polmateer shrugged again. "Perhaps. There were no witnesses, and your word is as good as his; but there are plenty around Mescal who believe Steve, and your reputation is against you. . . . Here's regards." He downed his drink and turned away.

Barry did not touch the drink Polmateer had bought. Face white with suppressed anger, he rolled a cigarette and was lighting it when two cowboys stepped to the bar beside him. They ordered drinks, and one of them addressed the bartender.

"Seen anything of Clay Dawn, Joe?"

The bartender nodded towards the room at the back. "Poker game."

"That's bad, Tuck," the puncher told his companion in a low voice. "The kid's got no right playin' poker with all that *dinero* on him. . . . Hey, Joe! How long has he been playin'?"

"Five, six hours."

"Who's sittin' in with him?"

"Steve Moley and a couple fellas from the Slash B." The bartender moved away in answer to a summons from Polmateer.

"That's all we'll get out of him," said the cowboy. "Tuck, what are we goin' to do about it?"

"Git drunk like we started out to. I ain't goin' to waste my time on Clay Dawn. Clay! They oughta called him *Putty*."

Barry moved away, glancing at the cowboys as he did so. He did not know them. Thoughts busy with what he had overheard, he passed through the doorway to the street. So Clay Dawn was in Mescal, and with a considerable sum of money. Barry had not known Clay intimately, but he remembered him as a boy who was rather weak of character. And when a weakling with a wad gets into a poker game—

He turned abruptly and passed around a corner into the passageway which led to the alley. Through the open windows came the sound of a piano and the nasal voice of the entertainers. The end window had its shade drawn down to the sill, so Barry moved to the rear of the place, sidestepped a pile of tin cans, and brought up outside a back window. The shade of this, too, was lowered, but a band of yellow light showed between its edge and the window sash. Through this space Barry peered.

Four men sat around a circular table, above which hung a ship's lantern. Stacks of chips and money told of a poker game, but at the moment play was suspended. One of the four—he with his right side towards Barry—had slumped over on the table, head pillowed on one arm. His hat had fallen off and lay on the floor. Across from him sat Steve Moley, who, together with the other two players, stared intently at the sleeper.

The one facing the window glanced furtively at Moley, received a nod of encouragement, and reached for the sleeper's coat. As he drew it carefully to one side, Clay Dawn—for Barry decided that the helpless one was he—raised his head and brushed an arm across his eyes. Mumbling something which Barry could not hear, he pushed back his chair and struggled to his feet. For a moment he stood swaying, arms working jerkily in time to the words he spoke in a voice now pitched high enough to carry through the closed window.

"Dam' crooks, tha's what you are! Wanna get my money. Well, you ain't gonna. I'm gettin' outside—" He turned towards the door which opened on the saloon, lurched forward a few paces.

The man facing the window got to his feet, and swift as thought raised an empty whiskey bottle and brought it down on Dawn's head. The young fellow pitched forward on his face and lay still.

Barry drew his Colt and smashed the lower pane with one clean swipe. Almost before the glass had ceased tinkling, he jerked the shade from its roller and thrust the gun through the opening.

The three stared at him, immovable, the one who had downed Clay Dawn crouching over his prostrate form.

"Get 'em up, all three of you," commanded Barry.

For an instant they remained hesitant, then reluctantly elevated their hands to the level of their shoulders. Keeping them covered, Barry reached through the opening and unfastened the window catch. Carefully he raised the sash until a click told him the pin had sprung into the top stop. Leaping upward, he lay for a moment balanced across the sill, then wiggled through the opening.

Inside the room, he backed to a corner where he could command every entrance. Somebody was thumping on the door, and Barry could hear the thud of boots rounding the alley corner. He addressed the man nearest the door.

"Let Ace Polmateer in."

Polmateer entered and closed the door behind him. "What are you up to now, Weston?"

"Helpin' you keep the Palace pure and unstained," drawled Barry. "I think you said somethin' about square games and no rough-house. Well, I looked through the window in time to see that jigger over there sock Clay over the head with a bottle. Knowin' you run a square joint, I horned in."

The two men measured each other, Barry's look challenging, Ace's calculating; then the door opened and a bouncer announced the arrival of the sheriff. Sam Hodge strode into the room and glanced about him importantly. "You, huh?" he grunted at sight of Barry. "What you done now?"

"Started where he left off five years ago," said Polmateer. "A few minutes ago I told him Steve's story of that old shooting, and he swore it was a lie. He broke in here, probably to get Steve."

"You're a bigger liar than Moley," said Barry flatly. "I was lookin' through the window and saw that jigger hit Clay with a bottle."

"What do you say about it, Steve?" asked Polmateer.

"He busted the window and poked his gun through it, orderin' us to put up our hands. Hop Finch grabbed a bottle, and Clay Dawn tried to take it from him. Hop hit Clay over the head. I figure it was a holdup."

"That settles it," said Hodge. "Give me your gun, Weston."

Barry stared at the sheriff, fighting the rage within him. "If you want this gun you'll have to come and take it."

"Better hand it over," came a slow voice from his right. Barry jerked his head around to see the face of one of Polmateer's gunmen grinning at him through the window. The fellow's gun rested on the sill, its unwavering muzzle pointed directly at Barry.

Resistance was out of the question. Steve Moley, after his humiliation at Barry's hands, would give much to see him under six feet of sod; Polmateer had no liking for Weston; Sam Hodge was sheriff by virtue of Horace Moley's money and influence. The cards were neatly stacked against him.

Barry holstered his gun. "Let's go over and see the judge. I'll pay the fine and get it over with."

"It begins with a J, but it ain't judge. It's the inside of the jug you're goin' to see. Come along."

Hodge took his gun and ordered him to lead the way

through the Palace. The crowd of drinkers and gamblers stared at him, their occupations for the moment forgotten, and six gaudily dressed and painted ladies whispered excitedly among themselves. Barry's unwilling attention was attracted by one of them. She was small and dark and undeniably beautiful, of Mexican extraction. As his gaze met hers he saw the lovely eyes widen slightly, the red lips part as a little Spanish exclamation escaped them. She came forward quickly, stood before Barry, forcing him to halt.

She addressed the sheriff. "W'ere ees eet you take heem?"

"To the calaboose. Move aside, Lola."

"W'at you take heem for?"

"Bustin' up a poker game—disturbin' the peace—attempted robbery."

"One man do all these! He mus' be ver' brave."

Steve Moley pushed forward and took her by an arm. "Come on, Lola; you're holdin' up the parade."

For an instant her eyes flamed as she looked up into his face. Steve was smiling, but Barry saw his strong fingers tighten about her arm, saw the girl wince slightly at the pain. Her lashes drooped and she permitted him to turn her aside.

Barry resumed his walk to the door, passed through the entrance to the street. One of Ace's gunmen fell in beside him, and with the sheriff following he strode down the plank sidewalk to the jail. Here he was thoroughly searched and locked in a cell.

Half an hour later, Hodge and the gunman reappeared carrying between them the limp form of Clay

Dawn. Barry watched by the light of the single lantern which hung in the corridor as they went through Dawn's clothes, then dropped him in the adjoining cell and locked the door.

The jolting he received partly revived young Dawn. As the two left the jail, Barry saw him sit straight up and look about him with wild, unseeing eyes.

"Crooks!" he mumbled thickly. "Tha's what you are —crooks! But you won't get it. Need it for Clement. Need it—to get him—outa—jail."

His eyes clouded and the words became a mumble which Barry could not understand. Finally Clay sank back to the floor and in a few seconds was snoring.

Barry seated himself on the edge of the bunk and ran his fingers through his hair. George Brent had told him that Clement had escaped; the wild words of this sodden youth would indicate that he had been apprehended. If Clement were brought back to Mescal they would hang him; the Moleys would see to that. Greatly disturbed, Barry tossed about until nearly dawn before falling asleep.

He was awakened by the sound of heavy footsteps in the corridor. A rough and surly individual had entered, bearing a pail of water and a bunch of keys. With one of the latter he unlocked the adjoining cell, and with the former thoroughly doused the still sleeping Clay Dawn, who awoke choking and swearing.

"Clear out," ordered the jailer. "Sleep it off somewhere else."

Clay sat stupidly gazing about him, then, upon being jerked to his feet, stumbled through the doorway and down the corridor to disappear from view. An hour later the jailer reentered the corridor and unlocked the door to Barry's cell.

"Front office," he said. "Somebody to see you."

Barry entered the room to find Sam Hodge and Horace Moley awaiting him. His belt and six-gun lay on the officer's desk. Hodge motioned towards it.

"Put it on and git out. Mr. Moley says to let you go."

The lawyer spoke crisply. "He also says not to come back. Weston, you left here under a cloud. You're no sooner back than you create a disturbance. We don't want you in Mescal. Get on your horse and ride—and keep riding."

"Suppose I don't want to leave?"

Moley's long face was very cold. "In that case you must suffer the consequences. You are a disagreeable person, Weston, with an unsavory past. I assure you we can make it very difficult for you."

Barry reached for his gun belt and buckled it about him; then he drew the weapon and examined it critically. Replacing it, he eyed them grimly.

"Mescal happens to be my home. If I ever leave it, it will be on a shutter."

"Even that," said the lawyer softly, "is quite conceivable."

He grinned, and it suddenly struck Barry that the long eye teeth of the man resembled greatly the fangs of a predatory wolf.

CHAPTER V

QUESTIONS WITHOUT ANSWERS

BARRY spent a fruitless hour in Mescal searching for Clay Dawn. He wanted to question that young man about his brother, Clement; the news that the elder Dawn had been captured worried him greatly. Among his boyhood friends he numbered Clement first; he was willing to go to almost any length to help him, especially so since he could not bring himself to believe that Clement would shoot a man without first giving him an opportunity to defend himself.

Failing to locate Clay, Barry rode to the Flying W. He found the supplies he had ordered piled against the back door, from which place his step-father had been too lazy or too indifferent to remove them, and proceeded to carry them inside and stow them away. His mother had had no breakfast, so he fixed something for her, then cooked a meal for himself and ate it thoughtfully.

It was clear that he was up against a neatly stacked deck. The powers that be had demonstrated right at the start their ability to finish anything he might start.

His arrest and detention had been intended as a lesson; his release was for the purpose of ascertaining whether he would profit by it rather than an admission that the case against him was weak.

Barry smiled grimly. He was no longer a green kid, he didn't scare worth a darn, and he had learned a lot about men since last they had known him. As for the gunmen of Steve Moley and Ace Polmateer, a gentleman named Colt, plus considerable practice and a natural ability, had rendered Barry capable of standing up to any of them. The lesson must go unheeded; his mother needed him, and he had a hunch the Cinchbuckle needed him too. Most decidedly he would remain and see things through.

He set about washing the dishes and cleaning up, then helped his mother to the gallery and saw her installed in her rocking chair. His step-father was not about, and he did not bother at this time to look him up. The thought of Clement in trouble kept haunting him, and at last he made up his mind to visit the Cinchbuckle.

Mounting, he rode over the flat basin rangeland, crossing the creek which bisected it. He was on Slash B territory now. Presently he forded the shallow stream which separated Moley's spread from the Cinchbuckle and headed for the ranch house.

It was mid-morning when he dismounted at the hitch rack. His halloo brought the cook, who informed him that Clay Dawn had not returned to the ranch and that Barbara was riding with the bank president, Alonzo J. Frothingham. He decided to wait.

Within the hour they appeared, riding slowly side by side. Barry stood up, hat in hand, waiting for them. Frothingham helped her from her horse and walked with her to where Barry was standing, the victim of a sudden strange shyness.

The slim, tomboyish Barbara he remembered had blossomed into a beautiful young woman. The brown hair was a shade or two darker, and he caught the reflection of dull bronze where the sunlight struck it. Her features were as he remembered them, only fuller, more softly rounded. The frank blue eyes regarded him in their old direct manner, but Barry thought he could detect a haunted, desperate light in their depths.

"Good mornin', Barbara," he said quietly.

Her voice was listless. "Hello, Barry. I heard you were back."

That was all there was to it. Just as though he had been gone a week instead of five years.

"Mr. Frothingham, this is Mr. Weston."

Barry for the first time took account of her escort. He saw a slim, immaculate man of indeterminate age, with light hair and eyes and a close-cropped mustache. His attire was of the latest Eastern pattern, with whipcord riding breeches and boots of soft leather. He smiled engagingly and offered his hand.

"Weston? Not the chap who spent the night in the calaboose?"

"The same," drawled Barry, his eyes narrowed slightly.

Frothingham laughed. "Pardon me for mentioning the subject, but it was such a glaring frame-up that it amused me. They had to let you go, of course. Clay's testimony would have knocked their case into a cocked hat. Your mother owns the Flying W, I believe; how is her health?"

"Poor; but I believe she will get well with the right kind of care. I aim to see she gets it."

"Of course you do! Well, I'm glad to have made your acquaintance. I am the president of our local bank, and I'm intensely interested in the basin ranches. Their prosperity means my bread and butter, and I want to work hand in hand with their owners. You have a nice spread, Mr. Weston, if it is properly managed. Should you need financial aid for improvements or repairs, call on me, won't you? After all, a bank makes money by lending on good security, and I'd ask none better than these basin spreads."

"Thank you, sir; I'll remember that."

"Do. Now I must bid you good-morning. Miss Dawn will want to talk with you, and I must be at the bank by noon. Good-by." He bowed to Barbara, flashed a smile that included both of them, and sprang lightly on his horse.

"He sure is different from most bankers," said Barry as Frothingham rode away. "I always thought you had to pry them loose from their money."

"Did you want to see me about anything special, Barry?"

Weston regarded the girl quietly. There was no warmth in her face and the blue eyes were openly hostile. Her attitude puzzled him; surely she must have forgiven him for that quarrel with Steve in her presence five years before.

"Yes, I did. Shall we sit down?"

She led the way to the gallery and indicated a chair. For a short space they sat there stiffly, for all the world like two strangers.

"You've heard about Clay?" he asked abruptly.

"Yes. Mr. Frothingham told me. Clay hasn't come home yet; I imagine he is ashamed of himself. As for you—"

"Yes?"

"I thought that perhaps after five years you had changed. You haven't. No sooner are you back than you go hunting for trouble."

Barry did not reply. Evidently the story that he had broken into the poker room to get at Steve Moley had reached and impressed her. A streak of stubborn pride possessed him. There would be no corroboration of his story that he had broken in to save Clay; young Dawn was unconscious at the time, and the others had lied and would stick to their lie.

"I reckon I'd better get right to the point," he said after a moment. "What's this about Clement bein' in jail?"

It was a brutal question, and it stirred her to the depths. The color left her cheeks, and her eyes went wide.

"Who told you that?"

"Clay. But he was in a stupor, and I didn't know whether he was speakin' the truth or not."

"It's true," she said tensely. "Clem got into trouble

about a year ago by shooting Cal Garth, one of Steve Moley's men. It happened behind the Palace and Ace Polmateer and his two bouncers were first on the spot. They kept everybody away until Sheriff Hodge arrived. He swore at the inquest that Cal's gun was fully loaded and in his holster."

"I reckon you know that's a lie."

"Yes. Clem would never do a thing like that!"

"I understood that he got away."

"He did, but—"

She broke off, and Barry spoke quietly. "I reckon you also knew that, with all my faults, I'm a friend of Clement's. Barbara, I want you to forget that you don't like me; I want you to tell me everything so that I can help him."

For a moment she regarded him, and he thought the tears were very near. Suddenly she spoke. "Yes, I know that. I'm going to tell you all. Two months ago Horace Moley sent for me and told me Clement was being held in Idaho for—for another murder, but that the matter could be fixed with money. I gave him a thousand dollars and told me I'd raise more. I went to the bank and Mr. Frothingham lent me two thousand dollars on a note.

"Last week Horace Moley said he must have five thousand more. I went to the bank again and mortgaged some more stock; then we rounded up what three-year-olds we had left, and Clay drove them north and sold them under the market for quick cash. We intended paying it on the notes, but you know what happened last night."

"Yes, I know. So you've paid Moley eight thousand dollars?"

"Yes. But it meant Clement's safety, and I'd sacrifice everything we own for that."

"Sure you would, Barbara, you don't know just where in Idaho Clement is bein' held?"

"No. I know nothing except what Mr. Moley told me. He is handling everything."

"Do you have receipts for the money you paid him?"

"Of course not. We can't put anything in writing. Barry, please don't interfere. He will handle it; he will get Clement free."

"There's another thing I wanted to ask you about. You've been losin' stock, haven't you?"

"We were short at the last roundup, and cattle have been going ever since. Not beef cattle, but breeders. Ike Wetmiller, our foreman, swears the rustling is being done by an outlaw named Tug Groody; but we've put night riders on the south and east lines for months at a time, and I would be willing to take my oath that no rustler has crossed our boundaries."

"I reckon you heard that I brought a dead man to town with me. He was shot on the trail by an outfit that must have been Tug Groody's. His name was Tom Slater, and they said he hung around the Cinchbuckle. What do you know about him?"

"He came here a year ago and told me he was broke. Wanted to use the south line cabin while he prospected. I let him have it. Since I heard of all that money he had I've been wondering if he wasn't in league with the rustlers."

"Probably; although five thousand dollars is a big cut."

"Is there anything else you want to ask me?"

"Just one thing more. Barbara, what is it that you hold against me? Why can't we be friends like we used to be?"

Her eyes flashed. "It's because of Clement! He worshipped you; the two of you were together all the time. That quarrel you started with Steve here on this gallery he carried on after you left. It was a fight with Steve that led to the one with Garth. Now he's in danger of his life, he has brought us worry and shame, all because of you!"

They were on their feet now, facing each other. Barry's jaws were set and he spoke almost harshly.

"He has brought you no shame! Worry, of course; but not shame. Because Clement would never do a shameful thing. Somebody reloaded Garth's gun and put it back into his holster. As for this story about his murderin' somebody in Idaho, I don't believe it."

"You don't believe it?"

"No. Why should Horace Moley work to get him out of trouble? Clem hated Steve, licked the tar out of him, killed his pet gunman. If Moley knew where he is, he'd move heaven and earth to bring him back here and hang him. The old lobo is bleedin' you—takin' your hard-earned money and robbin' your brother Clay in poker games so as to weaken the Cinchbuckle. I understand he wants the ranch; well, he couldn't think of any better way of forcin' you to sell than by takin' your money away from you."

Her face was flaming with anger. "You're talking about the man who is befriending us, who is going to save Clement for us! Remember where you are."

Barry controlled his anger with an effort. "I'm glad you reminded me. You ordered me off the spread five years ago. I had thought—hoped—that you had forgiven me. I see you haven't. But I want to say one thing before I go, and that is that I believe Clement is innocent and that I'm goin' to do my best to prove him so. I know Clement, and I'd back any play of his to the limit. I don't know Horace Moley, but I believe he's a crook and a liar and a blackmailer, and I aim to try to prove that too. And when I do, maybe you'll be ready to welcome me back to the Cinchbuckle again. Goodby."

He strode past her and down the steps. She followed him a short distance, her eyes wide and troubled. Almost, she called to him to come back. Then he was on his horse and riding swiftly away from the house, and she finally sighed and returned to her chair. But his words in defense of her brother stirred a little glow within her and made her ashamed of her own lack of faith in Clement.

Barry rode swiftly until the sweep of the wind had cleared his head and cooled the resentment which had flamed within him. He began to realize that Barbara was not to be too severely criticized for her treatment of him. Steve Moley had declared that Barry had fired on him before he could pull his gun; the quarrel itself must have appeared to her as inspired by petty jealousy; she did not know the truth about the fight in the Palace the night before. And she was quite sincere in her belief that his friendship with Clement had led her brother astray.

When he had branded Horace Moley as a blackmailer, he had spoken in anger; now, as he considered the matter, he began to wonder if he had not uttered the truth. The idea grew until at last he pulled his horse to a halt and sat staring across the rangeland. Barbara had paid the lawyer eight thousand dollars, and Clay had probably been robbed of another four thousand. Considering the depleted condition of the ranch, this loss should be a heavy one. And Moley did want the Cinchbuckle. If he wanted it badly enough Barry could easily conceive of his descending to any means to acquire it.

Barry shifted in the saddle and glanced about him. He had forded the little stream and was now on Slash B range. He carried his reasoning a bit farther. If Moley wanted to weaken the Cinchbuckle, rustling of its breeding stock would help. Barbara had guarded the south and east boundaries of the spread, across which rustlers would naturally be expected to strike. The north boundary was the creek which bisected the basin, on the far side of which lay the MB of Matt Billings. The Slash B bounded the Cinchbuckle on the west—and the Slash B was owned by Steve Moley. Granted that the Moleys were actually robbing the Cinchbuckle, Barry's conclusion was very obvious.

He rode on towards the Flying W, his alert mind searching for connecting links in the chain of circumstances which had been woven within the last year. The

Moley's had acquired their land craze just a year before; his mother had been taken seriously ill a year before; Clement Dawn had killed Cal Garth a year before; Tom Slater had occupied the Cinchbuckle south line cabin a year before.

According to Barbara, Slater had represented himself as a down and out prospector. Where did he get the five thousand dollars? Had he found gold or silver or some other valuable mineral? Barry had never heard of any precious metals being found in this section, but that was no argument against their existence. Barry's eyes narrowed with a sudden thought. Suppose Slater had found something valuable on the Cinchbuckle; suppose, being broke, he had gone to Horace Moley with the discovery; suppose Moley had bought him off for five thousand dollars!

It was a rather wild supposition, but it would explain much. It would explain the sudden land craze and would make more logical the theory of robbery and blackmail.

"By Godfrey!" exclaimed Barry. "I believe I've stumbled on it. There is somethin' on the Cinchbuckle that Moley wants—somethin' more valuable than cattle or land, somethin' that Moley must own the Cinchbuckle in order to get. If he wants the Flyin' W, it must be there too. But what under the sun is it?"

Back on the Flying W he prepared dinner for his mother and took her for her daily walk. The little lady was cheerful and seemed to be improving rapidly. He left her in her rocking chair and walked around to the building to the bunkhouse. The dinner hour was over, and his two hands should have been on the job long before this.

Opening the door he stepped inside. Chet Lewis and the two hands were playing cards. Barry watched them for a moment, then spoke quietly.

"You men can get your time."

Chet turned on him angrily, and Barry saw that his courage had been fortified by liquor. "Seems like you're takin' a lot on yourself, firin' hands I hired. They're on the payroll until I tell 'em to quit."

The two had dropped their cards and were staring at Weston. Barry, from force of habit, stared back while he fought down the hot surge of anger which his besotted step-father had aroused. Lewis, mistaking his silence, staggered to his feet and stood swaying by his chair.

"Gosh A'mighty uppity, ain't you? comin' back here and tryin' to run things. Big he-man from the north! Well, I ain't takin' no more sass from you. Sam Hodge slapped you in the jug las' night, and by Godfrey, I'll —"

He broke off, for Barry, turning quickly to the wall, had seized a quirt which hung from a peg. Whirling, he raised the leather whip, brought it down smartly on Chet's shoulders. The man squealed with pain and sudden fear.

"Hey! Don't you go a-doin' that! Quit it, dang you! *Ouch!*"

Again and again Barry wielded the quirt, while his step-father dodged and danced and squirmed to escape the lash. At last he covered his face with his arms and bolted for the door. He brought up against the frame, rebounded, and finally managed to stumble through the opening.

Barry turned to the two punchers and indicated the doorway with a jerk of his head. "Get goin'."

He followed them outside, paid them, and stood watching while they saddled up. Without a word they rode off, headed for Mescal. Chet had disappeared, having learned that Barry's promise of a quirting should he find him drunk had been delivered in all sincerity.

Barry spent the rest of the afternoon making some necessary repairs, then, after supper, helped his mother to her room and sat there talking. In the course of the conversation he learned much about the present personnel of the Basin ranches, the newcomers to Mescal, the changes that had occurred during his absence.

"I can't understand what came over your stepfather," she told him plaintively. "Chet used to be a right handy man and a steady worker. After you went away he changed. When I saw him cleanin' up the house yesterday I just couldn't believe my eyes. Where is he now?"

"Fallen from grace, lady. I told you he would. He was in the bunkhouse playin' cards with the hands. I fired them."

"Chet won't like that," she said.

"Chet will have to lump it then. Listen, lady. I've always put up with a heap from that step-father of mine, just because he is your husband. I'm still puttin' up with plenty, but the partin' of the ways is near." He looked at her earnestly. "Ma, just where does he stand in your affections?"

There was quiet dignity in the answer. "That doesn't matter, son. The thing is that he is my husband. I promised to love, honor, and obey him."

"I don't see how you can either love or honor a rum-soaked weaklin' like him," he said slowly. "And if you obey him, you'll wind up by signin' away every right you have in this ranch."

"No, I won't do that. This ranch was built up by your father and me. It is your heritage, and he can't take it away from you."

"He'll try hard enough. Ma, the loss of the ranch wouldn't bother me. I'm young and strong and I know cows. Sometimes it's better to be foreman of a big outfit than to struggle and sweat and worry over a small one of your own. But I sure would hate to see the fruit of your and dad's toil pass into Chet Lewis' lazy hands or Horace Moley's dirty ones. This is your home; no one else is goin' to have it while you live."

"If you want me to, Barry, I'll deed it over to you now."

He bent and kissed her. "Lord love you no! I said it was yours, didn't I? But I'll watch over it for you, and heaven help the gent who tries to take it from you!"

CHAPTER VI

NIP AND TUCK

AN HOUR later, when Barry was sure his mother was sleeping, he saddled up and rode to Mescal. He was not looking for trouble, but it was necessary to show Moley and Hodge that their threats did not worry him. Also he was anxious to secure a cowhand or two in order that his mother might not be left alone at the Flying W. Chet Lewis had disappeared, but he might return to the ranch during Barry's absence; and while Weston did not anticipate any physical violence on his part, a drunken quarrel might easily undo all he had accomplished toward the restoration of his mother's health.

He dismounted at the Palace and went inside. The place was crowded, with a long line of men ranged before the fifty-foot bar and dense groups surrounding the gaming tables. Barry spotted the two punchers from the Cinchbuckle whose conversation the day before had warned him of Clay Dawn's presence in town, and succeeded in reaching a place beside them. Evidently their determination to make the most of their day off had been realized; they seemed rather the worse for wear, but were still going strong.

He thought to pick up some information about conditions on the Cinchbuckle, but their minds seemed to be on other things, and their conversation was a muddle of horses, guns, and the girls they had known in their ramblings about the country. Quite suddenly they put their heads together and lifted their somewhat raucous voices in song:

> *"Oh, I onct loved Molly Magurder,*
> *My gosh, I loved her so!*
> *But she married a danged sheepherder,*
> *So I rode to Idaho."*

"Nip," said one of them, "you're off key. That there 'Idaho' sounded like a coyote wailin' at the October moon."

"Tuck, you're a heap better judge of liquor than you are of music," replied the one called Nip. "It was you that was off. If you don't believe me, take a look at Ace Polmateer glarin' at you."

"Glarin' at who?" demanded Tuck belligerently. "He'd better not be glarin' at me. By jacks, I never did like the dude. If he glares at me I'll walk over there and sock him on the nose."

"No you won't. That there's a pleasure I been reservin' for myself. You stay here; I'll go over and sock him."

"Sa-a-y, who was he glarin' at, anyhow?"

"You. But you're friend of mine, ain'tcha? Think I'm goin' to stand by and let my friends git glared at? Well, I should shay not!"

"Tuck, I got it! We'll both go over and sock him!"

"Two of us to that shorthorn? Nip, I'm su'prised at you!"

The ensuing argument was drowned out by a sudden burst of music. Barry saw that the end of the room had been cleared and was now occupied by half a dozen beribboned and painted damsels who swayed in unison and bawled the words of a popular ballad with voices which made up in strength what they lacked in culture.

Barry turned his back to the bar, and, resting his elbows on its surface, surveyed them. The girl, Lola, stood out like a rose in a patch of rag weed. She was watching him as she sang. Presently the music ended, and the girls broke formation and scattered about the room. Lola came directly towards Barry, seeming to glide rather than to walk, her soft eyes fixed on his face, the hint of a smile on the red lips. She halted before him and put a small brown hand on his arm. The pianist was thumping out a waltz.

"Well the tall *señor* dance weeth Lola?" she asked softly.

Barry grinned down at her. "Lady, I'm light enough on my own feet, but I'm sure heavy on my partner's."

The girl pouted. "I am sure you are not tell the trut'. Come; eet ees not often that Lola mus' beg for the dance."

Barry reached into a pocket and drew forth a dollar.

"I'm all out of practice, and I sure would hate to spoil your good opinion of me. Here's a dollar; spend it to celebrate your lucky escape."

She pressed the money firmly back into his hand. "I weel not accep' eef you do not dance. Lola ees not that cheap."

The cowboy, Nip, spoke up. *"Señorita,* I'm some hoofer myself. How about takin' me on for a fall?"

"No. Eef I do not dance weeth the tall *señor,* I'm dance weeth nobody."

She moved to a vacant table and threw herself sulkily into a chair. Ace Polmateer went over to her and spoke in a low tone, but she answered him so fiercely that he shrugged and turned away.

"Some li'l spit-devil," commented Nip admiringly.

Tuck answered. "Ain't she, though? Stranger, you sure chucked old man Opportunity plumb out the back door. They's fellas in this room that would give a eye tooth for one dance with that *chiquita.*"

"That's right," agreed Nip. "Lola's been twinin' 'em all around her finger. Even Steve Moley neck reins and single-foots when she whistles."

"There's another jigger I'd like to take a poke at," said Tuck. "He gives me a heap big pain in the k-neck."

"Keep your big mouth shut," warned Nip. "You're drunk."

"Sez you! When I'm drunk I can't sing worth shucks; and I sure can sing. Le's try that second verse." Heads together, they bellowed another stanza of their song:

"Oh, I onct loved Josephine Taylor,
I used to call her Jo;
But she married a bowlegged sailor,
So to Texas I did go."

Through the swinging front doors came Steve Moley and the two men who had been in the poker game with him and young Dawn. Barry was still standing with his back to the bar, and at sight of him Steve frowned and stopped suddenly, then resumed his way, the other two at his heels. Steve dropped into a chair facing Lola. His companions continued to the end of the bar, where they ranged themselves facing Ace Polmateer and ordered drinks. Barry slowly rolled a cigarette. Steve was talking earnestly to Lola, who watched him with sullen eyes. Presently he got up and moved away, and the girl joined the other entertainers on the platform to render another song.

This time when the girls separated, she came direct to Nip, who, like Barry, had turned his back to the bar. She smiled at him.

"You lak to dance weeth Lola, No?"

Nip nearly fainted. "Like to! Lady, I'd give both legs and a arm— Tuck, is this a dream?"

"I have a feelin' it's goin' to be a nightmare."

The piano was going. "Come," said Lola coaxingly.

"Whoop-ee!" yelled Nip, and seized her.

"Look at him," said Tuck disgustedly. "He don't know a fandango from a full house! Why, he'll tromp that li'l girl to death. Why didn't she take me instead of him?"

The music finally ceased, and a beaming Nip escorted

Lola to the bar for the customary drink. Barry moved slightly to make room for her. She stepped on the rail and called her order; then, glancing about quickly, she spoke from the corner of her mouth.

"Watch good w'en you leave, Señor Tall One. There are two who wait outside."

Instantly she had turned and was laughing at something Nip had said; nor did she pay Barry any further attention. Weston ordered a bottle of beer and drank it slowly, his eyes traveling over the face of the big mirror behind the bar. Ace Polmateer still stood at the far end of the counter, but the two who had entered with Steve were not in sight. Moley was standing at a faro layout watching the play.

Finishing his drink, Barry turned and looked carefully over the assemblage. There was no doubt about it; the two had vanished. The sheriff had come in, and Ace Polmateer was talking to one of his bouncers. Barry felt a little thrill of anticipation. The stage was set. He would walk out, there would be an exchange of shots, and, if they killed him, one would swear it was self-defense on the part of his companion. If he got his man, there would be a witness to testify that he started the fight.

He was seeking the best way out of the situation when four more men entered the saloon. Barry did not know them, but their leader was tall and lean and saturnine, and carried his gun in a tied-down holster. The group halted just inside the doorway and looked over the crowd; then one of them nudged the tall one and nodded towards Nip and Tuck. Instantly the whole group moved up to the bar, halting directly behind the two cowboys.

"I been lookin' for you two fellers," said the tall one.

Nip and Tuck slowly turned. The former spoke coldly.

"Well, it looks like you've found us."

"It sure does. I have somethin' nice to tell you. You're fired—both of you. You've carried this thing too far. You were due back at the ranch this mornin'. Ride out and get your warbags and your time, then you're through."

"Not on your say-so," scoffed Nip. "Miss Barbara hired us, Ike Wetmiller; she'll do any firin' that's to be done."

"She has. I took it up with her before I rode in."

For a moment the two stood glaring at the Cinch-buckle foreman, but Wetmiller had the advantage of numbers and position. Nip gave a final glare and turned back to the bar; Tuck followed his example. Wetmiller and company backed through the dorway to the street. They were taking no chances. Lola discreetly slipped away.

Barry glanced at Nip's face. The cowboy's mouth was set and his eyes glinted with anger. Tuck was talking to him.

"We mighta knowed it. Part of the game, Nip. One by one the old hands are fired or killed off until only me and you are left. Wetmiller's been waitin' for an excuse to fire us, and we, like danged fools, gave it to him."

Barry signaled the bartender and ordered him to

fill their glasses; then, as they turned frowningly on him, he explained quietly.

"I'm Barry Weston of the Flyin' W. I fired the only two hands on the spread and I'm honin' to get hold of two good ones to replace them. You boys suit me from the ground up. How about it?"

They exchanged glances. "What's your proposition?" asked Tuck.

"Regular cowhand wages and a chance for some excitement. I've been warned out of town, and right now two men are layin' for me outside the Palace."

The smiles were replaced by grins of anticipation. Again they looked at each other.

"Suits me," said Nip.

"Me too," said Tuck.

"You're hired. Now listen. I just overheard you say that the Cinchbuckle is gettin' rid of its old hands. How come?"

"Well," said Nip slowly, "we ain't much on carryin' news; but you're our boss now, and I reckon you'll do to ride the river with. It's true. For the past year Wetmiller's been weedin' us out on one excuse or another. He's got Miss Barbara buffaloed; she thinks him jest about the best cowman that's stepped along the pike."

"Is he?"

"Shucks! I've forgot more about cows than he ever knowed; but he's a driver, and he has been ridin' night and day tryin' to cut down rustlin'. She's found him on that south line at noon and at two in the mornin'. She ain't happened on him when he's sleepin' his head off under a tree."

"And how about this rustlin'?"

"Boss, you got me. Stuff keeps slippin' away, a few at a time. Breeders. Sure is raisin' Cain with the calf roundup. . . . About these fellas that are layin for you; sure there are only two of 'em?"

"That's all. They came in with Steve Moley."

"Hop Finch and Pug Parsons. You leave 'em to us. When you hear us sing, you come out." Before Barry could question or object they had stepped away from the bar, and, staggering slightly, made for the doorway. Barry glanced at Ace Polmateer. He seemed relieved at their passing.

Barry seated himself in a chair near the door and tilted it against the wall. Five minutes passed—ten; then faintly to him came the words of another verse of their seemingly endless song:

> "Oh, I onct lovd Annabelle Ambler,
>   The fairest of her sex;
> But she married a tinhorn gambler,
>   So I moved to Nueva Mex."

Barry got up, stretched, and turned through the swinging half doors. He had the strange feeling of expectant eyes fastened on his back. Stepping quickly to one side of the doorway, he dropped his hand to his gun and peered about him through the darkness. Nip and Tuck had told him to come out; just what he was expected to do he did not know. Two figures detached themselves from the shadows across the street and came towards him, lurching slightly. Nip and Tuck.

"Mount up and ride," said Nip, "The road is clear."

He picked up the reins and climbed to the back of a stocky bay. Tuck mounted a roan, and Barry, pulling the slipknot in his own rein, vaulted to the saddle. They pulled away from the rack and rode out of town.

"If I'm not too curious," said Barry, "what became of Hop and Pug?"

"They're layin' on their backs meditatin'," answered Tuck. "And Hop is dryin' out. He was hidin' behind the waterin' trough, and Parsons was around the saloon corner. Nip took care of him. I snuck up behind Hop and said *'Boo!'* so sudden that he jumped three feet. I grabbed him by the slack of the pants and spilled him in the drink; then I yanked him out, stuck my persuader against his spine and made him walk to the calaboose. Sam had some rope in his office, so we wrapped 'em up good and stretched 'em out where he would be sure to fall over them."

"Did they recognize you?"

"Sure. I even told Hop I hoped that cotton shirt he was wearin' would shrink up enough to choke him."

"I didn't have no trouble with Pug," grinned Nip. "I tickled him on the neck with my clasp knife and hissed in his ear: *'Señor,* mak won move an' I'm cut out from you gizzard and peen heem behin' you ears!' He come right along. . . . Le's sing, Tuck:

> *"Oh, I onct loved Caroline Bummer,*
> *And my heart with emotion was fired;*
> *She got hitched to a dry-goods drummer,*
> *So to Oregon I retired."*

CHAPTER VII

A MYSTERY IS SOLVED

IT WAS midnight when they reached the ranch. Barry furnished Nip and Tuck with blankets and told them to come over to the house for their meals. When they had turned in and were snoring, he rode to the creek and crossed it near the point where the stream which separated the Cinchbuckle and the Slash B joined it. He followed the east boundary of Moley's spread clear to its southern limit, and turned into the road which skirted the south hills. If Cinchbuckle and Flying W cattle were being rustled over the Slash B, they would have to cross this road at some point.

Slowly he rode back and forth, pausing often to listen; but nothing out of the ordinary happened, the only sounds which reached him were the chirp of crickets and the distant wail of a coyote. With the coming of dawn he was back on the Flying W. He had drawn a blank, but his hunch persisted. Rustling operations would not be conducted nightly; he might be forced to patrol that road for a week or a month or even longer before another bunch of cattle were driven into the hills. And that was just what he meant to do: ride the south boundary until his hunch was verified or he was convinced that the Slash B was innocent of collusion with Tug Groody and his rustlers.

He decided to say nothing to his cowboys until he had something stronger than suspicion to work on. When they had eaten their breakfast he ordered them out on the range to take a rough tally of the stock; then, after caring for his mother, he slipped into the bunkhouse and snatched a few hours' sleep.

The report which Nip and Tuck brought in at noon was far from encouraging. They had covered enough of the range to get an idea of what the final count would be. The cream of the herd was gone, the breeding stock suffering the most severely.

"Jest like the Cinchbuckle," said Nip. "Tug Groody realizes that every time he rustles a cow heavy with calf he's gittin' two animals for the trouble of messin' with one. And the calf would have no brand. Gosh; a fella could build up a right nice herd by jest takin' care of the mamma cow until her calf is weaned, then turnin' her back on her own range."

"Tug don't believe in turnin' nothin' back," said Tuck. "He rustles the pa too, and keeps the whole family together."

"It's strange nobody has discovered where he keeps them," observed Barry.

"Not so strange, when you figure the territory covered by them south hills. It would take a year to comb them proper. We spent a lot of time in there, and once in a while would find some cattle sign; but the trails always petered out before we reached the end of 'em. They'd be washed out by rain, or jest vanish on a rock flat or in a creek. There for a spell Ike Wetmiller had us in the hills more 'n we were on the Cinchbuckle."

Several days passed uneventfully. Nip and Tuck were kept busy with the range work; Barry divided his days between caring for his mother and effecting repairs to house and outbuildings and equipment. He slept when he could, and spent his nights patrolling the south road. And at last the rustlers struck.

He was riding parallel with the stream which separated the two spreads, being on his way to the south road. It was quite early—barely ten o'clock. The moon had just risen, and by its light he could see recumbent cattle all about him, and occasionally an animal still on its feet. Quite unexpectedly he detected, ahead of him and to his left, the distinct thud of hoofs.

He slipped from his horse and glanced about him. The range here was flat and barren of any hiding place, and the figure of a horseman would be distinctly visible for some distance. Realizing that unless he made himself less conspicuous he would be discovered, Barry forced his horse to lie down and crouched beside the animal.

He heard a low voice, followed by the bawl of a cow and immediately thereafter the splash of water. Cattle were being hazed across the little stream at no great distance from where he lay. Presently a horseman topped the bank, followed by several animals. The leader pointed the herd across the Slash B, passing so close to Barry that he thought he must surely be discovered. A flank rider appeared, but fortunately his attention was taken by some animals that showed an inclination to bolt, and again Barry was unobserved.

Doubting that he would be so lucky the next time, Barry stood up, got his horse to its feet, and, mounting, boldly took his place on the flank of the herd. If he were mistaken for one of the rustlers, he might discover where they were taking the cattle; if detected, he had an even chance of escaping in the hazy moonlight.

Across the Slash B they plodded, coming at last to the extreme southwest corner of the spread. The animals under Barry's eye slowed to a halt on the heels of those before them, and Weston became aware that the herd was being hazed into a corral. He went about his part of the work methodically, ready at any moment to turn and run for it should some hawk-eyed rider fail to recognize him as a member of the driving crew.

As the last of his charges passed into the inclosure, Barry drew his mount to one side of the gate, a short distance from the other right flanker. On the far side he could discern the forms of the point man and the two who had ridden the left flank. Two more came up with the drag and pushed the few remaining animals through the entrance, the gate to which was immediately swung into place. One of the drag riders spoke briefly, "Okay, boys," and Barry identified the voice as Steve Moley's.

The Slash B men wheeled their horses and trotted towards the ranch buildings, Barry still among them. Nobody paid any attention to him. Two men on his right were talking, and he knew them to be the ones he had discharged from the Flying W.

Moley called over his shoulder, "Fifty head, even. All she stuff, and each cow carryin' a calf. Goin' to be fifty little mavericks runnin' around pretty soon."

The rustling was no longer a mystery. Some time during the night Tug Groody would collect the animals left in the corral and drive them to a park deep in the hills. Here the calves would be born, weaned, and branded with whatever mark their illegal owners desired. It was possible that many of them were turned back on the Slash B to grow to respectable maturity under a clear, unaltered brand. In time Moley's spread should pay handsome dividends!

Barry contrived to lag behind, finally halting his horse altogether. As the riders were swallowed by the haze, he reined to the left and headed for the Cinch-buckle.

Two hours later his sharp knock brought a sleepy-eyed Barbara Dawn to the door. Quickly he explained. "I'll get the crew up while you dress," he finished. "If we hurry back there we can surprise Tug Groody when he calls for them."

Immediately thereafter ensued a scene of orderly confusion. Horses were caught up and saddled, men appeared with rifles and six-guns. Barbara came from the house, tight-lipped and eager-eyed. In a compact group they spurred out of the yard, Barbara and Barry in the lead, Ike Wetmiller and ten punchers behind them.

They rode hard, for dawn was not far away; and

presently Wetmiller and his men, their horses being fresher than Barry's, forged to the front. Barbara remained with Weston. Day was breaking when they reached the little corral on the Slash B, to find the Cinchbuckle crew lounging in their saddles, smoking and joking. Barbara rode swiftly beyond them, checked her horse at the corral, then turned to wait for Barry.

"We're too late," she said. "They're gone."

"Then we'll pick up their trail and follow them into the hills."

Ike Wetmiller laughed. "Can't pick up what ain't there. We've already looked. There ain't a fresh cattle track south of the corral."

Barry rode around the inclosure examining the ground. Wetmiller was right; save for the shoe marks of the Cinchbuckle horses the earth was unmarked. As he rejoined them, Wetmiller spoke again.

"To my way of thinkin' it's a poor joke to get a crew up in the middle of the night on a wild-goose chase."

"Cinchbuckle cows were driven into this corral not five hours ago," said Barry flatly. "I know it, for I was with the bunch that drove them."

"It's a bit strange that they didn't recognize you," said Barbara slowly, and Barry caught the note of skepticism in her voice.

"The moon was bright, but it was too dark to distinguish a man's features at any distance. Later on they must have got wise; maybe somebody saw me slippin' away. They must have come back and turned them loose. There are plenty of tracks leadin' to and from the corral."

"There naturally would be," said Wetmiller drily. "That corral was built to hold cattle."

"Cinchbuckle cattle?" asked Barry sharply.

"We ain't got nobody's word but yours that there were Cinchbuckle cattle in it."

"Do you need anybody else's word?" asked Barry gently.

Wetmiller shrugged. "If it was too dark for them to recognize you, it seems as though it would be pretty hard to read a brand."

"That's enough," interrupted Barbara. "We'll have no quarreling. Ike, take the boys back to the ranch. I'll be right along."

"Barbara, I told you the truth," said Barry when the crew had left them. "Fifty of your breeders were turned loose in that corral. They were driven here by Steve Moley and five of his men."

"The moon didn't rise until after ten. Do you mean to tell me that Steve's crew crossed to the Cinchbuckle and rounded up fifty breeders in the dark?"

"I didn't say that. It's my hunch that they were already rounded up."

"By my boys? Barry, you're carrying the thing too far!"

He shrugged helplessly. "Let's look inside the corral."

Within the inclosure they dismounted and studied the ground.

"You can easily see that there were cows in this corral right recently. Barbara, you must admit that."

"I do admit it, Barry. And at least one of these cows

wore a Cinchbuckle brand." She pointed to a hoof-mark which stood out plainly above the rest. "That print was made by a particularly stubborn brindle cow that I remember well. I'd know her track anywhere. But I just can't believe that my boys were mixed up in a plot to rob their employer. Ike Wetmiller is with them all the time, and they simply couldn't cut out a bunch of breeders and drive them to the Slash B boundary without his knowing it."

Barry smiled grimly. "I reckon the answer is pretty plain then."

Her eyes flashed indignantly. "You mean Ike Wetmiller—! Barry, I won't let you even suggest such a thing! Ike is as honest as the day is long. He's worked for us faithfully. If any of our boys were in it, Ike certainly doesn't know about it."

"It must have been goin' on for some time. Maybe you can figure out a way they could do it without his knowin', but I can't. Barbara, don't you realize that if the Moleys want this ranch of yours, and if you refuse to sell, they'll do anything they can to cripple it so that you will sell? I told you I believed Horace Moley is blackmailin' you. I still believe it. And I caught Steve rustlin' your cows. Is it too much to believe that Horace Moley, with all his money, could buy your foreman?"

"It is!" she cried. "Oh, I do believe you want to help me, but you always go at it the wrong way. You dislike Wetmiller—you came near to quarreling with him a few minutes ago—and so you try to turn me against him. It is just like that night on the gallery—with

Steve. You found him there with me, and you were—were jealous, and—"

"Just a minute, Barbara. I got to set you right on that point. It wasn't jealousy that forced the fight with Steve; it was the resentment that every decent man feels at seeing an innocent, sweet young girl in the company of a scavenger like Steve Moley. You didn't know him. I did. So did Clement. That's why Clem or myself would do again what we have done to drive him off the Cinchbuckle. I feel like I do towards Wetmiller because my common sense tells me he's helpin' steal you blind; and all the tales of his honesty and faithfulness that you can think up won't change me a mite."

For the space of ten heartbeats they faced each other, glances locked; then Barbara turned abruptly and flung herself on her horse.

Barry watched her ride away with a little feeling of pity. Loyalty to her foreman and her crew was inbred in Barbara; but he knew that this loyalty had been severely shaken, and to have one's faith disturbed invariably hurts. Presently he mounted and rode slowly towards the Flying W.

More and more the conviction grew upon him that the Moleys were after something of great value. What could it be? A thought struck him so forcibly that he exclaimed aloud. He remembered that Slater had represented himself to Barbara as a prospector. That Cinchbuckle south line cabin where he had lived for a year might yield a clue to the secret. Barry determined to investigate at the very first opportunity.

He did not see the figure which rose from the chaparral on the hillside overlooking the corral. Steve Moley had lain in waiting ever since his men had turned the stolen stock on the range. Some sixth sense had warned him on the way back that the number of men behind him had diminished by one. A hurried check-up had disclosed that there had been two men riding the right flank where originally there had been but one, and Steve was quick to realize that a spy had in some manner contrived to mix with them. The command to release the cattle had followed.

Now he stood looking after the vanishing Weston, his dark eyes glinting, his lips tightly compressed. Wheeling, he made his way to his horse, and riding him into the south road headed directly for Mescal.

Barry had a visitor at dinner that day. Matt Billings of the MB came riding into the yard just as Nip and Tuck appeared for their noon meal. The four ate in the ranch house kitchen, and after the two cwboys had departed Matt lighted his pipe and spoke cautiously.

"Got a letter from George Brent, up in Sheridan. He told me about the job you gave him, and he sure is tickled. Enclosed a letter for you, explainin' that he don't dare write you direct for fear Walt Bascomb might monkey with your mail. Here she is." He passed the envelope across the table.

Barry opened it and read:

Dear Barry, I am sending this to Matt because it got something in it that Horace Moley would give a right hind leg to know. Hired a puncher yesterday who knows

Clement Dawn. Worked with him in Cheyenne. Clem is there now, and I thought you might want to write to him. Also I reckon Barbara and Clay would like to know that he is safe and well.

Y'rs truly,   George Brent.

Barry re-read the part about Clement, then placed the letter in his pocket. "No answer," he said. "A little personal business that George didn't want Moley to know about. Much obliged, Matt."

"No trouble, Barry. Glad of the chance to git over. You see, Harry Webb and Jeff Hope and some others have been after me to run for sheriff against Sam Hodge. I sort of honed to know how you stand on the matter."

"I'm with you every jump," said Barry heartily. "Hope you beat the socks off of him."

"It'll be a job," admitted Matt. "But things in the Basin are goin' haywire, and if I am elected I sure aim to do one thing: go after Tug Groody and keep after him until I git him. He holes up somewhere, and if a fella looks hard enough and long enough he sure oughta be able to find him."

When he had gone, Barry walked over to the bunkhouse where his two hands were sitting on the bench, smoking.

"You boys haven't been over to the Cinchbuckle for your time," he reminded them. "Reckon you'd better ride over now. And while you're there, give this letter to Miss Barbara." He smiled a bit grimly. "I reckon there will be no answer."

CHAPTER VIII

THE HEAD LOBO SPEAKS

IT WAS still quite early in the morning when Steve Moley drew rein before his father's house. His face was set and inwardly he was seething. Tying quickly, he strode up the walk and rapped on the front door. It was opened by Horace Moley, still in dressing gown and carpet slippers. He took one look at his son's countenance and motioned him into the parlor.

"I'm glad you called," he said. "I was going to send for you. Tug Groody was here before daylight with the complaint that when he got to the corral there were no cows awaiting him. I thought it was quite clear to you, Steve, that there must be no hitch in our plans. When I order things done, I want my orders obeyed."

"They were obeyed," said Steve fiercely, "but there was a hitch just the same." He went on to tell of the drive the night before. "It's a good thing I turned them loose. Barry Weston would have followed a fresh trail into the hills, and gosh knows what he would have found."

Horace Moley's eyes had narrowed. "Weston, eh?

The fellow is becoming a nuisance. He must be dealt with—ah—severely."

"You had him in the jug once; why didn't you keep him there?"

"And you set a trap for him the other night and caught your pets in it. Next time perhaps you'll consult me before acting. Weston must go; but he must go quietly. We can't afford to take any risks until after election. Sam Hodge is under fire right now, and there is talk of running Matt Billings against him. I can take care of that, but only if Sam has a clean slate from now on."

"I'll say he is under fire," said Steve gloomily. "Folks are still gruntin' about him not bringin' in Tug Groody for that Slater Job. And they're beginnin' to realize that Sam hasn't done a thing worth doin' since he's been in office."

"We'll take care of that at the proper time. A bold stroke just before election will sweep him in again. Leave that end of it to me. You get Weston. With him out of the way we can have some chance of acquiring the Flying W."

"And the Cinchbuckle—how about that?"

"I am taking care of the Cinchbuckle," Horace told him calmly.

Steve made a fierce gesture. "Do you realize that time is flyin'? I tell you we've got to cinch this thing! Man, the thought of it is drivin' me wild! All those millions waitin' for us, and we keep feelin' and gropin' and pussyfootin'! If I was handlin' the thing I'd turn Tug loose and strip the spread to the bone, even if we had to slaughter the cattle to get rid of them. Steal 'em clean and they'll have to sell."

"It's a good thing you're not running it," snapped Horace. "You must remember that gaining possession is only part of the plan. We must be able to show a clean title afterwards. We can't keep the thing a secret for ever, and when people learn of it they are going to question our claim to every foot of the land. If we go after the Cinchbuckle hammer and tongs, they'll be sure to connect up the rustling with our acquisition of the spread."

"They'll question our claim anyhow."

"Of course; but if we are properly covered up they won't be able to prove a thing. Take this rustling: Weston alone knows that you had any hand in it. His unsupported word is no good. Here's another illustration: for two months I have been working on Barbara Dawn. I told her that Clement had been jailed for a killing scrape in Idaho, but that I could get him out of it by spending some money. To date I've got eight thousand dollars out of her, and considering the depleted state of the spread that leaves her pretty well strapped."

"Blackmail, huh?"

"Call it that if you like. But even if she should tumble to it, her hands are tied. She has no receipt for the money, and no witness has seen her give it to me."

"Eight thousand, huh? Added to the four we got out of Clay that makes twelve altogether. Not bad."

"That is another instance. Clay was dead drunk, and he couldn't swear what became of his money. Hop

Finch and Pug Parsons, however, must be taken care of. They know too much, and when we finally get possession we don't want any witnesses to hold us up for a big share."

"I got you."

"That's fine. Perhaps we can manage it so that they quarrel and shoot it out. One kills the other, and Sam takes care of the survivor. . . . Well, we will see. You run along and figure out a way to get Weston. Let him disappear or meet with an accident. It's your job; see that you do it well."

"And how about the rustlin'?"

"Definitely off."

"Tug is goin' to kick like a steer."

"Tug can kick all he likes; we're not going to risk our scheme for the sake of pleasing Tug Groody. The more he kicks, the better I'll like it."

Steve eyed his sire curiously, but he had learned by this time that the lawyer's mind ran in deep, swift channels, and he did not question further.

At nine o'clock, Horace donned his dusty black hat and made his way to the bank. A clerk greeted him respectfully, and Alonzo J. Frothingham personally ushered him into the private office.

"Well, Horace, how goes it?" he asked jovially.

"I was about to ask the same of you. Has the girl come to you for any more money?"

"Not a red cent. The little country lass has a bit of pride, Horace. I've urged her to restock, and tactfully offered to lend her the dough; but she refused to accept. Tough luck, isn't it?"

"It is. And it's all your fault. When I told you to become friendly with her I didn't mean that you should rush her off her feet. Since you have become a suitor, she naturally refuses to put herself in your debt."

"She's a cute little trick, Horace. I'm quite smitten."

"Al, you're a damned liar. I know you. You'll never be in love with anybody but Alonzo J. Frothingham— or should I say Bert Alonzo, society burglar and stock swindler?"

"Now, now, Horace! No dirty digs. I can toss rocks too."

"Don't try tossing any in my direction, or you'll go back to making little ones out of big ones. And you hate manual labor, Al."

Frothingham flushed slightly. "Right, old top. You have me where the hair is short. What's on your mind?"

"I want you to push this hand-in-hand-with-your-patron business. Matt Billings is thinking of running for sheriff. Encourage the movement. Be interested in the affairs of the ranchers. Lend them money. You know the line."

Frothingham grinned. "I'll say I do. On their success depends my prosperity, and so on. That all?"

It was, and Horace Moley said so and departed. The pulleys were well greased and the puppets were jumping. He was completely satisfied with himself.

His complacency received a rude shock that evening. As he was leaving his office, Barbara Dawn dropped from her horse and stepped up on the sidewalk.

"Good evening, Barbara," greeted Horace genially. "What can I do for you? But do come inside."

"No. I won't take but a moment of your time, Mr. Moley. I just wanted to know if you had heard anything more from Clement."

"H-m-m-m. Yes, I have. There is a little hitch: a stubborn turnkey who must be—ah—fixed. A thousand dollars should do it."

Barbara answered shortly. "I'm sorry, but I've gone the limit. The Cinchbuckle won't stand for another cent."

He cackled skeptically. "Now come, Barbara; surely you can raise a paltry thousand. Certainly your brother's safety should be worth it. I, myself, will be glad to lend you that amount on your personal note."

She eyed him in that level way of hers. "I thought you might suggest something like that. Mr. Moley, I called to tell you that I believe you have already robbed me of eight thousand dollars. I don't believe you know where Clement is. In plain English, I think you are a cowardly thief and blackmailer."

Moley gasped his surprise. "Why, you—you—! You're insulting and slanderous! I'll sue you for that statement and take every bit of your miserable spread away from you!"

She laughed scornfully. "With no witnesses, Mr. Moley? I thought you a shrewd lawyer! Listen to me. If you know where Clement is, you'd do everything in your power to bring him back to face that ridiculous charge you and your hired sheriff brought against him. I should have realized before that you have been playing on a sister's fear for the safety of her brother to wring from me every cent I possessed. You produce Clement, well and safe and with the charges against him removed, and I'll pay you that thousand dollars; otherwise, if you as much as suggest my giving you another cent, I'll use my quirt across your face."

Turning abruptly, she walked across the sidewalk, her heels clicking against the planks. At the rack she whipped the rein free, mounted, and rode away without a look behind her. Moley stared after her, rage and chagrin struggling for the mastery; then, with a harsh oath, he turned and walked jerkily towards his house.

He'd get even with this high-handed young lady for the manner in which she had spoken. And she should suffer through her own brother—both her brothers. She must have discovered where Clement was, otherwise she would not have been so outspoken; and if she knew, Clay knew too. And Clay was weak. Also he liked to gamble. By the time he reached his house the wolf fangs were showing in a sour grin.

Steve Moley, in the meanwhile, had crossed to the Palace. His father had given him a definite assignment, and a little liquid refreshment might help in the devising of ways and means of removing the inconvenient Barry Weston. There was not much doing inside; the gaming tables were deserted at this early hour and even Ace Polmateer was missing. One bartender looked after the wants of a scant half dozen drinkers, and the silence, after the raucous clamor of the night, was a bit oppressive.

Steve looked about him and saw the girl, Lola, seated

by herself at a table. She wore a colorful Mexican dress, and a single artificial red rose adorned her black hair; nevertheless, she looked sad and pensive. Steve signaled the bartender and seated himself opposite her.

"Hello, Lola," he greeted.

" 'Ello," she replied listlessly.

"Say, what's the matter with you? Why ain't you in bed?"

"I cannot sleep. Me, I'm not feel good."

"Huh. Well, here's somethin' to cheer you up. Down the hatch, *chiquita.*"

Lola set the glass on the table after the smallest sip of its contents. Steve eyed her suspiciously. "You sure are off your feed. You in love?"

"Loff?" She laughed bitterly. *"Quien sabe?"*

He leaned over the table. "Is it with me, kid?"

She surveyed him from beneath lowered lashes. "You want from mak me laff?"

"Nothin' funny about it. You'd better not let me catch you lovin' anybody else." A sudden thought struck him. "Sa-a-y, it ain't that lanky Barry Weston, is it?"

"Bar-ree Wes-ton?" she repeated after him.

"You know; that jigger Sam Hodge arrested. By jacks, I'll bet it is! You horned in then, and you'd never seen him before. And later somebody tipped him off— Lola, damn you, it was you!"

"You are talk crazee," she told him coldly. "W'en I'm see heem to teep heem off? I'm ask heem to dance with me, and he say no. Why should I teep heem off?"

"Because you're in love with him! Shove a fella six

feet in the air and slap a head of curly hair on him, and the girls go crazy."

She shrugged. "Ees my business to act crazee over many men. That beeg fat peeg you call Hop Finch, I pull hees ears lak he ees a dog and tell heem I'm lak heem so he ees buy many dreenk. An' the tall miner who ees call' Olsen, he ees ogly lak the cow; but he has moch gold, so I tell heem I'm lake beeg men. An' Steve Moley ees spend moch money on me, so sometam I'm tell heem I lak heem."

"So that's it, huh? It's the dough I spend on you that you like. Well, let me tell you this, you little cat—"

Lola laughed musically and shook her head. "He ees so fonny! An' he ees not theenk that maybe Lola talk jus' to mak heem an-gry."

Steve's ire died, and a slow grin came over his face. "You little devil, you! Don't you go playin' with me like that. Now drink up like a soldier, and then I'll have to go. Man over there I want to talk to."

He tossed off what was left of his drink and got up. At the far end of the room, slumped behind a table, was Chet Lewis. Steve sat down opposite Barry's step-father, eyed him speculatively for a moment, then motioned to the glass which stood before him.

"Drink up, and I'll buy another. You look like you need it. What's wrong?"

"Ain't nothin' wrong."

"No? How's that pet step-son of yours?" He saw Chet's eyes flame and laughed shortly. "Listen, Chet; I'm not wastin' any words. You hate the son, and so do I. You aim to pass up that quirtin' he gave you?"

"By Godfrey, no!"

"All right. Now listen good. That spread belongs as much to you as it does to anybody. I want you to go back there today. Tell Weston you're sorry; dig in and work like the devil—today."

"Steve, I won't do it."

"Yes you will. I want to get hold of Weston quietly, and have Tug Groody take him so far away he'll never get back. That means he must be nailed when he ain't expectin' it. You're the man to turn the trick."

Chet's bloodshot eyes showed a flare of interest. "How'll I do it?"

"Use your head for somethin' besides a hat peg. You'll be in the house with him, won't you? You ought to be able to find some way of puttin' him to sleep and tyin' him up. Tug will do the rest. Hang a lantern in the window and he'll come a-humpin'. All you got to say is that Weston rode away some time durin' the night."

Chet was fumbling at the stubble on his chin. "Mebbe I could manage it."

"Just think of that quirtin' he gave you and you can." Steve got to his feet. "Make it tonight. I'll get in touch with Tug."

Chet Lewis nodded jerkily and reached for the glass before him. With it half way to his lips he paused. When he went back to the Flying W he must go sober or Barry would quirt him out of the house. Besides, he would need all his wits. Maybe just a little nip before he pulled it off. He sat there frowning into space as he puzzled over the manner in which to render his step-son helpless.

Presently he got up and shuffled to Bascomb's store, where he purchased some shot and a buckskin bag. He poured the former into the latter and tied the poke with rawhide. It made a formidable weapon, capable of stunning without killing. That evening he ate supper at a restaurant, then rode to the ranch.

Barry was not at home, but Mrs. Lewis was seated on the gallery, and, using his head as Steve had suggested, Chet greeted her in a friendly manner and helped her to her room. He had prepared supper for her and was placing it on a tray when Barry entered the kitchen.

"So you're back. Where's ma?"

"I helped her to her room. I was jest fixin' to take these victuals to her."

Barry scanned the tray, found the food satisfactory. "Good enough. Take it in."

Lewis shuffled his feet embarrassedly. "Uh—Barry, I reckon I sort of got off on the wrong foot the other day. It was the liquor talkin'. I aim to pitch in and help you from here on."

Barry eyed him skeptically. Chet refused to meet his gaze, and Barry believed real repentance to be entirely out of character in this man.

"Let it ride," he said. "I'll meet you halfway any direction you jump."

A bit to his surprise, Chet washed the supper dishes and brushed about with a broom; so Barry spent some time reading to his mother. When she finally fell asleep, he went quietly about the house locking up. Chet was waiting for him in the living room.

"Barry," he said, "I'd sure admire to sleep inside. Now that I am to straighten out it ain't right for me to bunk with the hands."

"Suits me. You can take the spare bedroom."

Chet nodded and turned away. Once inside the room, however, his expression changed from that of almost servile docility to one of unleashed hatred.

"Danged upstart!" he muttered, and drew the bag of shot from his pocket. For a short while he fondled it, testing its weight, then placed it beneath a pillow and undressed. He lay on the bed in the darkened room, listening to the distant chimes of the living room clock as it tolled off the hours. Nine—ten—eleven—twelve.

Chet got silently to his feet, the bag of shot in his hand. Softly he opened the door and tiptoed into the hall. The room he occupied was between that of Barry and his wife's. He listened at the doorway of each in turn, knew from the sounds that both slept. Barry's door was slightly ajar; Chet touched it with a shaking hand, groaned inwardly with the realization that he could not go through with it yet.

Shuffling noiselessly to the kitchen, he felt around until he located the bottle of whiskey he had hidden there. From it he took a deep draught, wiped his lips nervously, raised the bottle again. The liquor warmed and exhilarated. Outside somewhere Tug Groody waited, he told himself. If he didn't make a good job of it a yell would bring him. He returned to his room, lighted the lamp, and hurried with it to the hall.

This time he did not hesitate. The lamp in his left hand, the bag of shot in his right, he pushed open the door and hurried to Barry's bed. He had decided that it would be impossible to surprise his step-son; nevertheless, he recoiled from the gun which emerged from beneath the covers.

"D-don't shoot!" he stammered. Then as Barry swung his legs to the floor, "It's your ma, Barry. I looked in at her a minute ago. Had a hunch somethin' was wrong. She was layin' there so still and white that I come for you right off. I—I'm afraid. You'd better look at her."

With an exclamation of alarm, Barry dropped the gun on a chair and sprang to his feet. Ignoring Lewis, he strode swiftly towards the door; and as he passed, Chet drew the shot bag from behind him, raised it swiftly, and brought it down on Barry's head with all the force he could muster. Barry, carried by his own momentum, staggered forward a stride, then his knees buckled and he plunged to the floor and lay still.

Quaking with a sudden fear, Chet watched the still form, the lighted lamp rattling in his shaking hand. With an oath, he placed the lamp on the washstand and sped silently to his room. From the chair on which he had placed them he took a coil of rope and an opened clasp knife. Pausing only long enough to assure himself that his wife had not been disturbed, he ran to Barry's room and proceeded to bind him securely, completing the job by gagging him with a scarf.

Back in the kitchen he lighted the lantern and set it on a window sill. Apprehension gripped him. Suppose

Tug did not come? Suppose the two new cowhands noticed the light and came over to investigate? Sweating with fear, Chet seized the half empty bottle and raised it to his lips. A slight sound on the step outside brought him sharply erect, staring.

The door opened and Tug Groody stepped into the room.

CHAPTER IX

GOOD FISHING

ALONZO J. FROTHINGHAM sought out Matt Billings the day after his talk with Horace Moley. He timed his ride so as to arrive at the MB at noon when he would be sure to catch Matt at the dinner table. Billings immediately invited the banker to join him.

"Ain't often I draw a bank president to eat with," grinned Matt.

"If I had my way the opportunity would be yours quite often," replied Frothingham. "I want to know you Basin ranchers better. It is your patronage which keeps my bank operating. We should work together; your problems should be my problems."

"You don't want mine; they're too numerous and heavy."

Frothingham raised his eyebrows. "Surely not so numerous and heavy that sufficient capital could not eliminate them."

Matt laughed grimly. "Oh, no. If I had ten thousand dollars cash I could do somethin'; but I'm shy of that amount by some nine thousand, eight hundred and fifty."

"Why haven't you come to me?"

Matt nearly swallowed his knife. "Huh? Never thought of it; didn't figger it would do any good. I ain't got no bonds to put up for collateral."

"You have something more valuable than bonds, Mr. Billings. You have a lifelong reputation for honesty and square-dealing. I'd rather lend my money on such collateral than on all the gilt-edged bonds in the world."

"That's funny talk from a banker!"

"Is it? Maybe I'm a funny fellow. Tell you what I'll do. I'll lend you ten thousand dollars on your own note."

"Who'll I git to endorse it?"

"Nobody. Give me a mortgage on this place. Personally I wouldn't require even that; but we do have to adhere to some banking regulations. I want to see this Basin thrive. I can't raise cows myself, but I can get behind the men who can."

Matt eyed him steadily, his weathered cheeks slightly flushed. "Say, Mr. Frothingham, you're a man to tie to! That means I can build up my herd, make some repairs— Say, you ain't jokin', are you?"

"Not at all. If you want ten thousand dollars with this ranch as security, come into the bank tomorrow morning and we'll fix things up."

"By Judas, I'll do it! Say, this calls for some celebratin'. I got me a jug of blackberry wine some folks back East sent me five, six years ago. We sure will sample it right now."

"There's another thing I wanted to see you about," said Frothingham a bit later. "I've heard it rumored that you intend to run for sheriff at the next election."

"I'd figgered some on it. Jeff Hope and Harry Webb and some of the others have been proddin' me. But I don't reckon it'll do much good; Sam Hodge has got Horace Moley and his money behind him."

Frothingham took a couple of cigars from his pocket and politely handed one to Matt. "Mr. Billings, I consider it your duty to run. Look here: I've been in Mescal a comparatively short while, but anybody can see with half an eye that Sam Hodge is—well, let us say inefficient. Take that Slater case. Barry Weston described the ones who waylaid and shot him, and we are agreed that the guilty party is Tug Groody. The rustling on the Cinchbuckle and the Flying W is also blamed on Tug. Sam has his description and knows that he hangs out in the south hills; but what has he done about it? Nothing; absolutely nothing. I tell you, we need you in the office of sheriff, Mr. Billings, and I for one am ready to back you to the limit."

Matt's face was tight. "If I was sheriff, you can bet I'd camp on that jigger's trail until I got him."

"That settles it. You'll be our next sheriff. If you need any campaign funds, come to me. We'll have to fight trickery with trickery. If Sam starts a vote-buying campaign, we'll boost the ante and beat him at his own game."

"I'm buyin' no votes," said Sam flatly.

"Of course not. Others will take care of that for you."

"No, sir, they won't. I won't stand for it."

Frothingham eyed him in mock admiration. "Mr. Billings, you impress me more and more. But if we don't buy votes, we'll use the money for propaganda. We'll have to educate the people who vote honestly. You draw on me for what funds you need; I'll advance them on your personal note."

That was, in effect, the end of the matter. They talked for some time and consumed a quantity of blackberry wine; but Frothingham had said what he wanted to say, and he took his departure as soon as he could gracefully do so. Matt gripped his hand and told him haltingly how much he appreciated the loan which Frothingham was about to make him.

The banker laughed. "Forget it, Matt. I'm not doing you any favor. I'll make money for my bank through the interest you pay. I'll draw up a demand note which I can call and renew from time to time when you have a little spare cash. That will protect me and won't hold you to payment on any definite date. Drop in tomorrow and we'll fix it up."

Once out of sight of the house and its grateful occupant, Frothingham chuckled. "The old geezer swallowed it, hook, line and sinker. I hope the others are as easy."

Not knowing of Barry's disappearance, he stopped at the Flying W on his way to the Bar 70 of Harry Webb. He found Mrs. Lewis on the gallery, which she was now able to reach by her own efforts.

"I don't know where Barry is," she told him. "Chet

says he rode away sudden last night. You might find him at the Cinchbuckle."

"I'll see him some other time," smiled Frothingham, and rode on. The smile vanished as soon as he had turned his back. The thought that Barry might at that moment be enjoying the company of Barbara Dawn was not a pleasing one.

He reached the Bar 70 about mid-afternoon, and was fortunate enough to find its owner repairing a corral fence. They sat down on a log and chatted for a short while, the conversation finally turning to Matt's candidacy.

"I've about persuaded him to run," said the banker, and went on with the line he had given Matt about the inefficiency of Sam Hodge. He still clung to "inefficiency," but Harry Webb was not so particular of his language.

"Sam's a danged crook; always has been and always will be. Between him and Horace Moley, they about run the town. Horace wants to buy my place, but I'll see him in Tophet first, much as I'd like to clear out."

Frothingham looked about him. "You have a nice spread, Mr. Webb; why do you want to leave it?"

Webb shrugged. "I don't like the climate. Jerry Weston and me was old friends. I've seen his widow rustled blind. Last year Charley Dawn died, and now the Cinchbuckle is on the down grade. Matt lost everything through sickness. George Brent was closed out by your bank. That leaves just Jeff Hope and me."

Frothingham spoke earnestly. "I had something to do with the Brent case, but that was before I knew how things stood. Between you and me I'll say that I was stampeded into taking action against Brent. I've bitterly regretted it ever since, and I'd give a lot to undo what has been done. You Basin ranchers are my bread and butter; I want to work hand in hand with you."

Once started, he spread it on thick. Harry Webb, at first skeptical, became interested, and interest in time became conviction. This Frothingham was a right decent hombre; he seemed sincere in wanting to help. And it was true that only by aiding the ranchers could he expect to profit himself. Harry wound up accepting Frothingham's offer to lend him five thousand dollars, the deal to be closed the following afternoon.

"I'd just as soon you didn't mention it to anybody," said Webb as they parted. "I'd made up my mind to get out, but that five thousand will enable me to do what repairin' and improvin' the place needs, and also to help Matt a bit. If he's elected things will be different; if he ain't, I'll sell out and settle with you."

"Don't think of it," begged Frothingham. "We can't lose." He neglected to mention, however, just who he meant by "we."

Jefferson Hope also proved to be an easy victim. All the ranchers had been hit by the two years' drought, and all of them needed ready cash. Astute enough in the breeding and selling of cattle, they were apt to be a bit hasty in accepting a man's word; for here in the West a man's word was his bond. Honest and square-dealing themselves, they measured others by their own standards. Frothingham was a banker and apparently very sincere in his efforts to secure their cooperation. That line about their well-being meaning his own prosperity appealed to their sense of logic. Here, they decided, was a go-getter—a man courageous enough to back their game and stand or fall with them. In the parlance of the range, Alonzo J. Frothingham would do to ride the river with.

Jefferson Hope, of the Anchor, was caught by the banker at the tag end of a particularly disheartening day. He was a sad-faced man, with a pair of handle-bar mustaches which accentuated his appearance of gloom. Alonzo J. had supper with him, and when he finally left, Jeff's eyes were moist as he hoarsely thanked him for allowing him to borrow ten thousand dollars, the cash to be delivered two days hence.

"You can bet I'll git behind old Matt," he declared earnestly. "I aim to spend some of that *dinero* where it'll do the most good. Matt wouldn't think of buyin' a vote, but we fellas will sure take care of that. We'll put him in office and bust Sam Hodge and Horace Moley right loose from their eye teeth."

Besides the Slash B, which, of course, was not on his schedule, Frothingham had missed one Basin ranch on his visit. That was the Cinchbuckle. For one thing, it was out of his way; for another, he knew that Barbara would not borrow any more from him. The knowledge piqued him and at the same time stirred a vague feeling of admiration for the girl.

"Anyhow, she's hooked for seven thousand," he consoled himself. "I guess that's all I can get for her, unless Horace thinks up something else."

Horace had thought of something else. When Frothingham returned to Mescal he went to the Palace. Horace Moley was standing at the bar. At a table sat his son, Steve, and young Clay Dawn. A little adroit fishing had convinced Steve that Barbara had not mentioned him to her brother in connection with the rustling, and the burden of his conversation at the moment was that he had not been to blame when Clay was struck over the head, and that the young fellow had lost his money honestly. Steve felt it his duty, however, to give Clay a chance to win it back, and would be glad to hold himself at young Dawn's disposal.

Frothingham stepped to the bar beside the lawyer, greeting him as one casual friend would greet another. When the bartender was out of earshot Moley whispered, "What luck?"

Frothingham chuckled. "Excellent. The suckers are biting today, Horace. Ten thousand each to Billings and Hope, and five to Webb. Weston wasn't home and I did not have time to visit the Cinchbuckle."

"No need to visit it. Steve is talking Clay into another poker game. When Steve leaves, you might stop for a word or two. Clay is part owner of the Cinchbuckle, and any debt he contracts is binding on the whole outfit. He might accept a loan where the girl would refuse."

They parted almost at once, Horace Moley hurrying to his supper, Frothingham to the table occupied by Clay Dawn, Steve having sauntered away. The boy mechanically waved an invitation to the banker to join him. They talked a while over their glasses, then Alonzo J. came to the point.

"I was over to see Matt Billings this morning. He's going to restock and put the MB on its feet again. I'm glad of it; would like to see all the Basin ranchers do the same. Take the Cinchbuckle; it's a beautiful spread, well watered and well grassed."

"You should have said *greased*. The cows slip away fast enough."

"We're going to remedy that. Matt Billings will run for sheriff; with him in office I've an idea the rustling will cease."

"Fat chance he's got."

"He has a very good chance. The people in the Basin are awaking to the fact that Sam Hodge is not the man for the job. Webb and Hope are backing Matt with real money, and I am going to take a little hand myself. My interests are tied up with those of the ranchers; I aim to work hand in hand with them for the betterment of the community."

Clay had heard it before, but it still sounded convincing.

"I'd like to help the Cinchbuckle," said Frothingham, "but being interested in your sister puts me in a difficult position. I don't want to risk offending her by offering to finance the ranch, and I know that her pride would prevent her accepting any offer I might make. You're different; you're a man and I can talk with you straight from the shoulder. Incidentally, you're a partner in the enterprise, and there is no reason in the world why you should not accept a loan from me."

"Barbara wouldn't stand for it," Clay said slowly.

"Is it necessary that she know of it at once? Surely you are discreet enough to handle money of your own. You can put it in a little at a time, and when you have built up sufficiently to justify your action, you can tell her about it. You can repay me when you are making money again."

Dawn's eyes were glistening. "Sounds reasonable."

"It is reasonable." Frothingham looked at his watch. "After banking hours, but I have a key and know the combination of the vault. Let's run over and fix it up now. How much can you use?"

"I'd better start off easy like. Say a thousand."

"Better make it two. You can't do much with one."

So another fish was netted. Clay, blood tingling, his reluctance to take the step without consulting his sister smothered beneath a sense of his own importance, duly signed a demand note which he was assured could be renewed at any time, and departed with two thousand dollars. Steve Moley was waiting for him outside, and repeated his offer to let Clay get even. The boy, suspecting nothing, and really believing his luck must turn, accompanied Moley to the poker room, and soon was plunged deep into a game with Steve and two companions.

Alone in the bank, Alonzo J. Frothingham, alias Bert Alonzo, sat back in his swivel chair and grinned at the upper northwest corner of the room.

"Good fishing," he murmured, and rubbed his hands delightedly together. "Very good fishing indeed!"

CHAPTER X

TUG SETS A TRAP

NIP AND TUCK, in accordance with Barry's instructions, came over to the ranch house for breakfast to find a disheveled and triumphant Chet Lewis in command of the kitchen. Chet had emptied the bottle, and his courage had risen accordingly.

"Barry went away last night and left me in charge. You fellas can roll your blankets and vamose. You're through."

For a moment they stared at him, then exchanged significant glances.

"That's funny," said Nip. "Barry left Chet in charge, Tuck."

"Yeah," agreed Tuck, "Chet's the big boss now."

"And he said we're fired. Seems like we can't hold a job a-tall. . . . You start the fire and I'll rustle some breakfast."

"You ain't eatin' here," declared Lewis. "I said you was fired."

"He said we was fired," repeated Tuck.

"That's what he did. . . . Rustle that wood; I'll

be slicin' some bacon." Nip went to work, talking as he sliced. "You know, Tuck, some fellas are right funny. And forgivin' too. Now you take Barry Weston; he just whopped the devil out of that ornery step-father of his, then turns right around and makes him boss of the spread."

Chet's bloodshot eyes were blazing with wrath. Lurching forward, he grasped Tuck by the arm and swung him away from the stove. "I said to git out, dang it!"

Tuck examined him curiously. "Nip, I do believe our new boss forgot to wash his face this mornin'."

Nip came up to them and peered eagerly into the wrathful countenance of Barry's step-father. "Danged if you ain't right! Can you imagine the boss of a nice clean cow spread like the Flyin' W goin' around with a dirty face? Grab holt, Tuck."

Before Lewis knew what was happening they had seized him and raised him from the ground. Twisting, kicking, and cursing, he was borne from the kitchen. There was a watering trough near the horse corral, and half a dozen feet away from it they halted.

"One—two—*three!*" counted Nip, and Chet Lewis described a short arc through the air and landed with a splash in the trough. As his head emerged from the water it was promptly pushed below the surface again, an operation which was repeated until Chet was cold sober and gasping for breath.

The two cowboys stood back and watched while he dragged himself from the trough and stood shaking with cold.

"It might help," said Nip, "if you told us just where Barry went."

"I d-don't know; he d-didn't s-say."

"Build a fire in the bunkhouse and dry out," said Nip. "Eat your breakfast there too. It's danged funny that Barry rode away without sayin' anything to us about it."

"Somethin' haywire," growled Tuck. "Somethin' awful dawg-gonned haywire."

They ate breakfast; then, remembering Barry's mother, went to some pains to fix a meal for her. To her question concerning Barry's whereabouts they lied cheerfully, assuring her that they knew all about his absence and that they expected him back soon.

They worked industriously, cleaning up and washing their dishes, then went outside, perplexed and worried. Smoke from the bunkhouse chimney told of a wet and bedraggled Chet Lewis. They questioned him again, but Chet, knowing that the preservation of his hide depended upon his entire ignorance of Barry's whereabouts, stuck to his story that Weston had awakened him during the night and told him he was riding away on some business, cautioning him to look after the ranch until his return.

"Our firin', then, was your own idea?"

Chet sullenly admitted that it was.

"Then we're hired until Barry says different. You look after Miz Lewis, fella, and if you even speak to her uncivil we'll make you hard to find."

Barry's horse was gone, and they examined the ground about the corral carefully. It told them that he had departed in the company of at least six others. Nip shook his head worriedly.

"I don't like it, Tuck. Let's ride to town."

"He'll show up. Trouble with us is we got the willies. Let's sing."

> *"Oh, I onct loved Elizabeth Bender,*
> *She made my heart flutter inside;*
> *But she married a cross-eyed bartender,*
> *So to Kansas I did ride."*

They found Mescal quiet, with but a handful at the Palace. Among them was the girl, Lola, seated as before at a table in a corner of the room. She smiled invitingly, and the cowboys, after giving their orders, joined her.

"The tall *señor,* Bar-ree Weston ees not come weeth you?"

"No, he didn't." They exchanged uneasy glances, then Nip explained. "To tell the truth, Lola, we don't know where he is. He disappeared last night."

"Deesappear'?" They could not mistake the sudden alarm in her voice.

"Yes. We got a hunch he's in trouble."

To their surprise she laughed shrilly, adding quickly in a low voice, "Order another dreenk; the bartender he ees watch us."

Nip was telling a funny story as the bartender served them. When the fellow was once more out of earshot, Lola spoke softly. "Why do you theenk these?"

"He's got enemies: Horace Moley, Steve, Sam

Hodge, Hop Finch and Pug Parsons. And he had a mixup with Tug Groody over that Slater jigger."

Her laughter rang out as though at something droll he had said. Lola was an excellent little actress. "You mus' go," she told them in the next breath. "'Me, I'm can't laff moch more. I weel fin' out and tell you. Go."

They went.

"You reckon we can trust her?" asked Nip.

Tuck flashed him a shrewd look. "Sure we can. Ain't you got no eyes? The li'l gal is in love with Barry."

For a moment Nip stood staring, complete overwhelmed. "She loves him, huh?" he said dully. "Aw, shucks! I mighta knowed it." In a low voice he improvised:

> *"Oh, I onct loved a gal named Lola,*
> *The sweetest gal in town;*
> *But she married a cowman named—"*

He broke off. "Weston don't rhyme with Lola, does it? Aw, shucks! Let's ride."

When they returned to the ranch, Chet Lewis had disappeared. It was just as well, for the two cowboys, in examining Barry's room, found his gun on the chair. Convinced that Chet knew more about the disappearance than he had divulged, they would have resorted to sterner methods than questioning to force the truth from him.

Around noon they saw a rider approaching at a fast lope.

"It's a gal," announced Tuck. "Must be Barbara."

"It ain't Barbara's horse, and this gal has black hair. Tuck, as sure as cats are growed-up kittens, it's Lola."

Lola it was. She rode up to them and swung lightly from her horse. Very neat and trim she appeared in her riding habit, but they found no time for compliments. Her dark face was tight, and the black eyes fairly glittered.

"I'm fin' out w'ere he ees," she said tensely. "Tug Groody 'as heem."

"Where abouts?"

She waved toward the south. "I'm not know from sure. We mus' look."

They dashed for their horses and in a moment were speeding over the rangeland. Glancing over his shoulder, Nip saw her following and waved to her to turn back. She did not obey, and he finally halted and turned.

"You can't go along," he said. "This is a man's job."

"Was eet man who tell you w'ere he ees? Come; we are was' tam." She spurred by him and took the lead, headed southward.

At that moment the one for whose safety they feared was seated on the ground beneath a scrub oak under the watchful eyes of six outlaws. For over ten hours they had been in the saddle, and now they were resting.

Barry had returned to consciousness to find himself tied over a horse like a sack of meal. At his cry they had halted, and he was permitted to ride erect with his feet lashed together beneath the belly of his mount.

Shortly before noon they had halted at the place where he now found himself. The horses were watered at a nearby spring and hobbled, a camp was established, and the men, not having stopped for breakfast, attacked the food they had brought with them.

Barry was not long kept ignorant of his fate. The men talked while they ate, and presently their conversation turned to him.

"How do you aim to rub him out, Tug?" asked a man with one arm in a sling.

"Lose him," replied Tug, who was fishing peaches from a can. "Lose him beneath a couple tons of rock in the gully over there. You know how loose them rocks are on top. Well, Mr. Buttinski is goin' to have a accident. Him and his horse and rig are goin' to git buried under a landsdide."

"Goin' to shoot him first, ain't you?" asked one of them callously.

"Shootin' makes too much noise."

"Hang him then," said he with the sling. "Hangin's quiet."

Tug stabbed another peach. "I been thinkin' some of it." He turned his baleful gaze on Barry. "Danged jigger beat us outa five thousand bucks."

Barry lay back on the ground and closed his eyes. So they had known that Slater had five thousand dollars on his person. Had Tug paid it to him and then murdered him to get it back? He dismissed the thought and concentrated on a plan of escape. His feet were bound, and one end of the rope which secured them was tied to a tree. With his hands free he could work loose, but not in the daylight, and by the way they talked he'd never see another night. He tried to reconcile himself to his fate and found it difficult. He was young and strong and eager for life; to lie here and await his end passively was impossible.

"We'll rub him out this evenin'," announced Tug. "I'm dog tired, and we don't want to hang around here after it's over. Turn in and git some shut-eye, boys. Each stand guard one hour." He named the order in which they were to watch.

Barry opened his eyes slightly. The men were composing themselves on the ground, and Tug, with a wide yawn, stripped off his gun belt and hung it on a projecting stub of a limb. The man assigned to watch seated himself twenty feet away from Barry and leaned against a tree. A rifle lay across his knees. Barry closed his eyes again, but before them remained the vision of a dangling gun belt with the butt of a big Colt projecting from the holster. It was careless of Tug to hang it there; or did he believe it out of Barry's reach? Weston determined that, given half a chance, he would have it in his hands. If he must die, it would be on his feet like a man.

The hours passed without the opportunity he awaited. At the end of each trick his guard would rise and, watching him carefully, would kick an outlaw into wakefulness to take up the vigil. It wasn't until Tug himself was aroused that Barry had his chance.

The big outlaw got up sluggishly, his eyes apparently heavy with sleep. Taking the rifle from the guard, he sank down on the ground and rested his head against the tree. Barry, watching him from beneath half closed lids, saw him close his eyes momentarily, then open them with a start. Getting slowly to his feet, Tug shuffled over to where Barry lay, and Weston, feigning sleep, felt the man's searching gaze bent upon him. Then came the sound of retreating footsteps, and he knew Tug had returned to the tree. The outlaw leader sat down with a grunt, and Barry opened his eyes. Tug was leaning against the tree trunk, head tilted forward, hat brim drawn low.

For what seemed an eternity Barry lay there motionless. At any moment Tug might arouse himself and call the others; still he dared not make a move until he was sure Tug slept. Presently he ventured moving about a bit. Tug paid no attention. Rolling to his left side, Barry doubled his legs and felt about his ankles for the knot. He found it, began working at the hard rope.

He made slow progress. In an agony of suspense he clawed at the knot, fingers numb, nails broken and torn. His eyes were fixed on Tug; should the outlaw awake now it would be all over with him. But Tug's position remained unchanged, and the gentle rise and fall of his shoulders suggested slumber.

The rope gave slightly, and Barry redoubled his efforts. The knot loosened, dissolved. He moved his legs, disengaged his ankles from the coils. He was free!

Almost was he tempted to crawl away into the shelter of the woods, but the dangling gun drew him. Its possession might mean the difference between life and death. Quietly he got to his knees, steady gaze fixed on the outlaw leader. Planting one foot firmly on the ground, he rose to his feet. No movement of any kind from the prostrate outlaws. A soft step in the direction of the tree from which hung the belt—another; and still no evidence that he had been observed. Three more swift strides, and his hand was on the walnut butt of the gun. In the act of drawing it he froze. Tug Groody had raised his head and was watching him, and Tug was grinning!

In that one swift moment Barry saw the trap which had been so skillfully baited. The other outlaws were awake and watching him, and he saw that several of them held their guns. They had never intended to hang him, but, desiring an excuse for shooting him, had hung the gun where they knew he could reach it. As in those other instances when he had stood face to face with death, Barry felt suddenly cold and calm and very sure of himself.

Tug Groody's rifle swept around in a short arc, six-guns snapped upward to line themselves on his form. Barry jerked the big Colt from its holster, leaped sideways, and thumbed the hammer. A futile click! He jumped again and snapped the hammer a second time. Another click! Tug Groody's grin was wider than ever, and Barry suddenly knew the reason for it. Tug had planted the gun there to tempt him, but he had first removed the cartridges!

Thus far not a shot had been fired. Barry's two swift leaps had disturbed the aim of the outlaws, who were still lying flat on the ground or resting on an elbow.

Tug was the man he had to fear most; Tug, with that deadly rifle which followed his every movement.

In that instance Barry thought very clearly. His action was the result of a sudden complete comprehension of the situation rather than a logical analysis of it. They had expected him to turn and flee, and their minds were set on shooting him as he ran. Instead of turning, he sprang directly at Tug Groody. One great leap he took, covering half the distance which separated them; and as he landed, he flung the six-gun at the outlaw leader with all the strength he possessed.

The rifle cracked, and the bullet struck him in the right breast; then the heavy Colt crashed against Tug's forehead and he sagged down like a pole-axed steer.

The shock of the bullet stopped Barry momentarily, but even as his mind grew hazy he realized that safety lay in keeping going, although his life blood was welling up in his throat to choke him. Carried on by sheer determination and power of will, he plunged blindly past the prostrate Tug, stumbling over vines, plunging through the brush like some stricken wild animal. Guns roared as outlaws hastily rolled and fired; lead shrieked through the air about him or thudded into the trunks of intervening trees. Two slugs struck him, but he was only dully aware of their impact. A gash in the earth opened before him. He could not have stopped had he wanted to. He plunged over the edge of the gully, fell some twenty feet, struck shale and rolled and slid to the bottom.

From the lip of the gully came shouts which his dazed mind could not comprehend. They were shouts of triumph and savage glee. They had him where they wanted him; he had obligingly stumbled into the very gully they had marked as his grave. A rock came bounding and leaping down the incline to strike within inches of his head. A small avalanche of stones followed it.

Consciousness lingered for a moment longer; desperate, pain-stricken eyes flitted about, the desire to live temporarily clearing a mind that was rapidly fogging. There was a projecting ledge some four feet from the bottom of the gully; if he could reach it, lie under the projecting overhang—

Barry called forth every effort of his will, got his legs and arms in motion, clawed and pushed and fought himself clear of the rubble. Slowly and painfully he worked his way to the ledge, the rocks raining about him like huge hailstones. Under the overhang his strength left him; he heard as in a dream the thud of the stones as they rattled down, but his eyes were closed and he was not conscious of the fading light which told of the closing of the aperture through which he had crawled.

Tug Groody, the sweat of mighty effort blending with the blood from his cut forehead, looked down on the mass of rock and stone and shale which covered the bottom of the gully and shook a hairy fist in the direction of the body they concealed.

"Lay there, dang you! Lay there and rot!"

"Tug!" cried a companion. "Listen!"

Tug jerked erect, turned his head. From some distant point came a faint but distinct shout: *"Barry! Barry!"*

Groody snapped into action. "Git goin'! Catch up the horses. Rustle, I tell you!"

They scattered. Swiftly they found their mounts, tore off the hobbles, threw on saddles and headstalls. Blankets were swept up deftly rolled, rifles were thrust into scabbards.

"How about Weston's horse?" asked the man with the sling.

Tug swore. "Leave it. Hurry, dang you! Scatter and meet at the hangout. Git goin'."

They were none too soon. Hardly had the last hoof-beat faded when Lola and the two cowboys came crashing through the brush. Their horses were lathered and panting, the riders scratched by chaparral and bruised by the branches they had struck in their headlong charge. They drew rein on the trampled ground of the camp, guns poised, keen eyes searching.

"Too late," said Nip. "They're gone. I heard a horse off to the right."

"And I heard one to the left. Nip, they've scattered. Look! Here's the rope where Barry was tied."

"Dios!" came an agonized cry from Lola. Her finger was pointing to the ground, her eyes were wide with horror. "Look! Ees blood!"

Tuck peered in the direction indicated and spoke gravely. "She's right. Blood it is. You reckon Barry got loose and shot it out with them?"

"What'd he use for a gun? His is home on the chair."

Lola had swung to the ground and was following the red blotches like a bloodhound. Her face was strained and white; her eyes burned like those of some primeval savage. Wonderingly Nip and Tuck dismounted and followed—followed straight to the edge of the gully. Here everything was plain.

Nip swore a horrible oath. "They've killed him and buried him in the gully! The sons of dogs!"

Lola was already sliding and leaping down the steep incline. They followed, helped with frantic hands to tear aside the rocks.

Presently Lola ceased her labor and spoke pantingly. "Eef he ees there," she pointed to the middle of the gully, "he ees los'. May be he ees crawl to the side."

They attacked the rocks closer to the wall of the gully, rolling them to one side, digging the shale away with their hands. It was Lola who finally crawled through the aperture they uncovered, Lola who cried out that she had found him.

"Is he—dead?" asked Nip anxiously.

"He ees still breathe! Ah, thank the Blessed Virgin! But we mus' get heem out—queek!"

They worked their way to the top of the gully with the unconscious Barry, gently laid him on the ground. The girl, suddenly calm, worked over him, sending Nip for water, telling Tuck to tear up his shirt for bandages.

Three wounds there were: pistol wounds in leg and shoulder, and a clean hole through the right lung. The first two were superficial; it was the rifle wound which had taken its toll.

Lola worked steadily and swiftly, cleansing the hurts, plugging them and applying compresses to stop the bleeding. She was white to the lips, and her eyes glowed like living coals; but her hands were steady, her touch deft.

"Ees all I can do," she said at last in a small voice. "He mus' 'ave the *medico* and he mus' be move' to a bed; but oh, so carefully."

"Fine!" said Nip. "We'll tie him on his horse and take him to the Flyin' W."

"No, no! You weel keel heem! You mus' tak two poles an' a blanket an' mak w'at you call the—the—"

"Litter?"

"Yes. An' you mus' walk weeth heem to the Cinch-buckle. An' you mus' be so careful or he weel bleed to death. Me, I weel ride for the *medico*."

Nip helped her to her feet and stood for a moment holding her hand.

"Lola," he said gently, "you'll sure do to ride the river with!"

She smiled faintly, the soft eyes misty. "Ees nice compli-ment for dance-hall girl, no?"

"I mean it. If you ever need an extra arm or laig, or even a head—"

"Aw, shut up," said Tuck gruffly. "That head of yours would only be a handicap to her. Come on; let's fix up that litter."

They carried the unconscious man until it was too dark to see, then camped in their tracks, alternating in watching over him. Lola had warned them, and they were careful to keep him well covered during the night.

If pneumonia set in, Barry Weston's slight chance of recovery would vanish like snow before an April sun. In the morning they took up their task, plodding steadily through the chaparral, cursing each other fervently at each misstep. Dusk had again descended when they finally staggered out of the hills to the Cinchbuckle range. Here they found waiting a spring wagon, the Cinchbuckle crew, Lola, Barbara, and the doctor.

The latter examined the patient carefully, nodding approval of Lola's handiwork. "Good job," he commented shortly. "I won't touch him until we get him to the house. Put him on the mattress, boys."

Ike Wetmiller designated three of his men to carry out the order. Nip and Tuck, weary to the point of exhaustion, had sunk to the ground.

Barbara addressed them quietly. "You will ride in the wagon with him. In the morning you can take two of my horses and go back for your own."

Late that night the doctor finally straightened and looked at the two girls who stood at the foot of the bed. "His chance is mighty slim," he told them gravely. "Somebody must be with him night and day."

"I weel stay," said Lola quietly.

Barbara's chin went up. "We will both take care of him."

CHAPTER XI

THE BETRAYAL

THE news of Barry's abduction and rescue reached Mescal that same night. It was brought by Ike Wetmiller, who, although not in the deal, had a shrewd suspicion as to who was behind it.

The crowd in the Palace hung on his words and questioned him closely. Who had shot Weston? Why? Where had it happened? How had Lola been drawn into it? Two within the Palace knew part of the answers, and their eyes instinctively sought each other. One was Steve Moley; the other, Chet Lewis.

The reaction of the first was disappointment, chagrin, and hot anger, with the latter predominating. It was clear that Lola had betrayed him; the little hussy had led him on, twisting him skillfully about her finger, wheedling from him information that he gave because he thought she cared for him. He was a fool; it was Weston she loved. The knowledge was like raw vinegar on an open sore.

Chet Lewis was the victim of but a single emotion: fear; stark, frantic fear. In his craven mind he was convinced that his part in the affair was known. It would be but a matter of minutes before those two hellions, Nip and Tuck, would seek him out and demand an accounting. Steve Moley was passing his table on his way to the door, and Chet clutched at his coat with desperate fingers, halting him and drawing him down into a chair.

"Steve, you heard what Ike said? Barry knows it was me that slugged him. He'll kill me sure!"

Moley's lips curved scornfully. "Don't be a fool. He's in no shape to kill anybody."

"He'll tell them two hands of his and they'll jump me. Steve, what'll I do?"

"Why ask me? It's your funeral."

"It ain't! You were in it too; you put me up to it!"

Steve surveyed him coldly. "You're crazy. Everybody knows he quirted you. You turned him over to Tug to get even."

"But—but—"

Steve got up. "See a lawyer," he sneered, and walked away.

Chet was completely overwhelmed by the immensity of the catastrophe. Steve had deserted him, and folks would believe exactly what Steve said they would. Try as he might to shift the blame, the fact remained that it was he who had delivered Barry Weston into the hands of the outlaw. He got up and hurried into the friendly darkness lest Nip and Tuck find him there.

For a moment he stood peering about him helplessly. Steve had said to see a lawyer. A sudden inspiration seized him; he'd go to Horace Moley and tell him the whole story. After all, Horace was Steve's father.

Moley received him in faded dressing gown and carpet slippers, and led him into the living room. "What do you want?" he asked curtly.

Chet told him, the words tumbling over each other in his excitement. It was Steve's fault. Steve had asked him to do it. And he had carried out his part of the agreement. He thought they were going to take Barry away and warn him never to return; instead they had shot him, and he, Chet Lewis, was an accomplice. But so was Steve; Steve—

Horace cut him short. "What am I supposed to do about it?"

"Why—why seein' as you're Steve's father, I thought—"

"Blackmail, eh?"

"No! No! I don't want money. All I want is to know how to git out of this. You're a lawyer; you can tell me what to do."

"But you could use some money, couldn't you?" Moley's voice had softened, and his eyes were narrowed calculatingly. An idea had just occurred to him.

"Why—why, yeah, Horace; a fella can always use money. 'Specially since I'll have to skip out of Mescal. But I—"

"I will give you one thousand dollars. Get as far away from Mescal as you can, and stay away." He unlocked a small safe and took out some bills which he counted and handed to the wide-eyed Chet. "I'll draw up a demand note for you to sign; if you come back I'll use it to put the fear of the Lord into you."

Within the next quarter of an hour Lewis was riding away from town. Steve saw him come from his father's house, and questioned Horace about it as soon as he was admitted.

"What did you do with that weak-kneed sister?"

Horace told him.

"You're crazy to throw away the money. He ain't worth it."

"The Flying W is," purred his father. "Don't forget the note, Stevie. It isn't worth the paper it's written on as far as he is concerned, but his wife has a peculiar sense of honesty. I'm quite sure she'll honor it."

"A thousand bucks won't break the Flyin' W."

The old wolf chuckled. "We shall see, Stevie." As ever, he was reticent regarding his plans. "At any rate it will serve to keep Lewis out of the way."

"There are a lot of others we'll have to put out of the way if we want to dodge trouble after we get control."

"Not too many," said the lawyer complacently. "The only ones to be eliminated are those who can connect our acquisition of the property with any—ah—irregular methods we may have used to acquire it. You and I, Stevie, are the only two who know about the big secret. The others are puppets, dancing when I pull the strings. Ike Wetmiller knows about the rustling, but he thinks you were behind that, and he can't talk without implicating himself. Hop Finch and Pug Parsons know that Clay Dawn was robbed; but that, too, was your affair. Sam Hodge knows nothing except that it is my money which keeps him in the sheriff's office. Frothingham will have his nest nicely feathered, and besides—well, he won't talk. But Tug Groody knows that I initiated the rustling scheme, and that means Tug must go."

"He'll be a tough one to get rid of."

Horace grinned at him. "We shall see, Stevie; we shall see."

"Dang you! Why don't you talk plain?"

"I enjoy my little surprises. You must humor me."

"How about Barry Weston?"

"Guesses a lot, perhaps, but knows nothing."

"He's dangerous just the same, and he's danged hard to kill." Steve made a sudden impatient gesture. "The whole thing's gettin' too complicated for me. If you'd loosen up I'd know what you are aimin' at. I tell you I'm gettin' the willies. With all that stuff just within reach and us not darin' to touch it!"

"Easy does it, Stevie. You like to gamble; you've learned by this time that when you hold good cards you mustn't let your face or your actions betray you. You play them close to your chest. This, too, is a game; only the stakes run into the millions. Think of it, Stevie— millions; *millions!*" His wolflike face was aquiver with avarice, his lean form trembled.

The fever communicated itself to Steve. He spoke through dry lips.

"Yeah, millions! Oh, I know we've got to play it careful; but when I think that somebody might stumble on the thing, I start to shake. How much longer do we have to wait?"

"At least a couple months. We must take care of the Cinchbuckle; Matt Billings and Harry Webb and Jeff Hope must have time to spend the money they borrowed from Frothingham. The Cinchbuckle is our keenest problem. Get to work on Clay Dawn. He's in for three thousand. When he is drunk he talks. Work on him. Find out if you can where Clement is hiding."

Steve got up, his lips tight. "He's waitin' for me at the Palace now. He's lost so much that he has to win right soon or go to Barbara with the whole story. He keeps tellin' Frothingham he's puttin' the money in the Cinchbuckle."

Horace went to the door with him. "Play them close to the chest, Stevie. It won't be long now. We'll soon be in a position where we can have anything we want— gratify every wish, every ambition."

The lawyer had another visitor that night. He came about two in the morning, when even the Palace was dark save for the poker room where Clay Dawn was being scientifically stripped of his borrowed cash. Horace awoke to a scraping noise on the window pane. Without lighting a lamp, he found his way to the kitchen door and unbarred it. A man stepped through the opening, his form looming large against the starlight. Horace closed the door and turned.

"Well?"

"We ain't run nothin' off for a month," said Tug Groody. "The boys are startin' to kick."

"Let them kick."

"Can't afford to. Horace, I got a nice little bunch of fellers together. I sure would hate to see them split up. And to keep 'em together I got to find work for them to do."

"Barry Weston got wise to our game; we can't risk it again."

"Lots of other ways, Horace; we don't have to depend on Wetmiller or the Slash B."

"Tug, if you rustle another cow, you'll do it on your own responsibility. I can't afford to be associated with you; it's too dangerous."

"I aim to go ahead alone then. I ain't never told nobody that you was behind the thing, and the boys are wonderin' if I got cold feet."

Moley's eyes narrowed. "You haven't told them, eh?"

"No. Why should I give you credit for runnin' the show when I can keep it myself?"

"You're quite right. Naturally it would help keep your men in line. Well, if you're determined to go ahead, there's nothing I can do about it; but it must be entirely on your own responsibility."

"You'll keep Sam Hodge off'n us?"

"Unless you go too far. Sam has this election to think of."

"I know. I'll run it careful. I've built up a nice little business, and I'd hate to see it git away from me. So long, Horace."

For some time Moley lay in bed looking at the dark ceiling above him. Tug had not told; nobody but Tug knew that Moley had been behind the rustling. It simplified things greatly. That bold stroke which was to land Sam Hodge in office for another term was shaping up nicely.

Once again his slumber was disturbed. At four o'clock there came a thumping on the front door. Horace opened it to admit Steve. Before he could reproach his son for arousing him, young Moley was speaking.

"I got what I was fishin' for! Clay passed out; it's gettin' to be a habit with him. I wanted to work on him some more, so I took him to the hotel and put him to bed. He started mumblin' in his sleep, somethin' about what Clement would say if he knew how much money he'd lost. I talked back to him, and he answered me. Then I got a hunch. I said, 'Clay, this is Barry Weston. I want to get in touch with Clement; where is he?' For a minute he didn't answer, and I sure thought I was out of luck; then, right sudden, he sat up in bed. 'Clem ain't in jail,' he shouted. 'He's safe; safe in Cheyenne.' Then he flopped back on the bed and took to snorin'."

Horace was as excited as his son. "Cheyenne, eh? That's in Wyoming. I wonder if we can depend on that."

"Why should he pick out that town unless Clement was there? I tell you it's a safe bet."

Moley made his decision quickly. "Get in touch with Sam Hodge the first thing in the morning. Tell him to be at my office at nine o'clock, ready to ride. And tell him to keep his mouth shut."

At the Cinchbuckle the stillness of death was in the

air. The bunkhouse was silent, not because of any respect for the man who lay so desperately ill in the rambling building a stone's throw away, but because the members of the crew had long since retired. A light burned in the room that had been Clement's, and on the bed lay a figure very still and white and helpless.

On one side sat Barbara Dawn; on the other, Lola. The Mexican girl was holding one of Barry's hands between her small brown ones, and her burning gaze was fixed on his face with an intensity which seemed designed to draw him back from the brink upon which his spirit tottered. Lola's face was haggard, and the little lines which loose living had etched on her olive skin were intensified by the strain; yet in that moment the watching Barbara thought her beautiful. The boisterous, brazen dance-hall girl was gone; the woman of the world had become the Madonna. Lola, whose habit had been to laugh at love, had ironically become its victim.

Barbara experienced a little stir of resentment, resentment which was quickly tempered with pity. The poor girl had not slept for forty-eight hours; she had ridden hard and fast, first to lead Nip and Tuck to Barry's assistance, then to the Cinchbuckle and to Mescal for the doctor, and again to the south hills and back. But for her Barry would not be here now.

She got up softly and went around the foot of the bed. Lola did not appear to have noticed her. Gently she placed a hand on the girl's shoulder.

"You are tired out, dear; you must rest. Go into my room and lie down; I will stay with him."

Lola shook her black head jerkily. "No. I mus' stay. You go."

Barbara persisted. "There are other nights ahead of us, and days too. One of us must be fresh and ready to take up where the other leaves off. Go and get a little sleep, Lola. Please."

Reluctantly Lola removed her gaze from Barry's face, turned her somber dark eyes on the girl who stood by her. She smiled wanly.

"You are ver' good; but I could not sleep. You go. W'en the morning she ees come, I weel geev heem to you." The smile became slightly bitter. "Me, I'm use' to sleep in the day tam."

So Barbara went; but she was too restless and disturbed to sleep. After tossing about for half an hour she got up, slipped into kimona and bedroom slippers, and tiptoed softly down the hall to the open doorway. There she stopped. Lola had bent her head over Barry's lax hand. Her cheek was pressed against the firm skin and she was crying softly. Barbara could see the tears glistening where they had fallen on his wrist. She turned quietly away, her own eyes misty. The resentment flared up within her again. What right had this girl to usurp a place which she felt to be hers?

She stole into her room and dropped to the edge of the bed. For a long while she stared through the open window at the starlit sky, and her thoughts, strangely enough, were on the days when she had been a tomboyish girl of sixteen and Barry a gangly lad of nineteen. She remembered again that night when she sat on the gallery with Steve Moley. She knew now why

Barry had fought with Steve that night. It had been to protect her good name. And now, after five years he had come back to fight for her again. And she had received him coldly, had repulsed his efforts to aid her.

She slipped to her knees, her clasped hands resting on the window sill. "Oh, God," she earnestly prayed, "be good to him. Let him live."

Much comforted, she got into bed and, after a while, slept.

Promptly at nine that morning, Sam Hodge entered Horace Moley's office. At three minutes past nine he emerged, a warrant tucked into an inside pocket. Riding a strong chestnut gelding, and driving a pack horse before him, he started for Cheyenne and Clement Dawn.

CHAPTER XII

SAM'S BOLD STROKE

AS though Barry's critical injury and dramatic rescue were the signal for a temporary cessation of activity, a period of comparative quiet descended upon the Basin. The seventh son of a seventh son might have read in this peaceful interlude the calm which precedes the storm, but none in the Basin were given to prophecy.

There were a number of good reasons for this stagnation, the chief one being that a certain passage of time was necessary to the culmination of Horace Moley's plans. Matt Billings, endowed with new enthusiasm, was carefully investing his ten thousand in improvements to his spread. Harry Webb and Jefferson Hope were equally industrious, and in addition were spending quite a sum in behalf of their candidate for sheriff. They used their borrowed money cheerfully, convinced that they could prosper only by placing in office a sheriff who would protect their herds.

Tug Groody was at large again, rustling indiscriminately from all the Basin spreads. Not even did he spare the Slash B, and Steve complained bitterly to his father against this deflection of their onetime ally. The elder Moley had rubbed his hands and smiled as though entirely satisfied.

"Let him go, Stevie. His robbing of the Slash B will do much to kill any suspicion that he might have worked for us. There is a saying somewhere about furnishing a man rope in order that he may eventually hang himself. Let Tug have all the hemp he wants."

With this Steve had to be content; but he knew his father well enough to realize that the old lobo had something up his sleeve which he would in his own time and manner divulge.

Sam Hodge had departed suddenly and nobody seemed to know his destination. Somehow the impression grew and spread that he was on a still hunt for Tug Groody, a rumor which Horace Moley carefully fostered. Even the deputy whom Sam had left in charge was ignorant of his whereabouts. He answered inquiries with a knowing wink, which merely added weight to the conclusion already formed. The days rolled by into a month, the month into two, and still there was no word from Sam. Folks endured the rustling phlegmatically in the belief that Sam was stalking his man. They expected him to strike at any moment.

Barry Weston, meanwhile, lay for days in Clement's bed at the Cinchbuckle, weak, delirious, despaired of at times by the doctor who attended him. Only the skillful ministrations of his two nurses kept him from slipping across the Great Divide. One of them was with him constantly. Nip and Tuck alternated in helping them and caring for Barry's mother.

The strain told on both girls, but their energy never flagged; they drew him from the brink time and time again seemingly by their very determination to save him. Lola had become quiet and subdued, and she seemed never to tire. Barbara, every bit as earnest, nevertheless came to accept the Mexican girl as her pattern. When she found herself on the verge of collapse, a glance at Lola through the bedroom doorway invariably gave her the strength to continue. For hours the dance-hall girl would sit patiently by Barry's side, holding his hand, stroking his forehead, crooning to him in Spanish or singing a quaint little Mexican lullaby to soothe him.

On one of these occasions Barbara heard a soft step at her side and turned her head to see the cowboy, Nip. He met her gaze with a wan smile, but the look in his eyes haunted her for many a day. Nip loved the Mexican girl with the whole big heart of him, but never before had he permitted Barbara to see it. She pressed his arm sympathetically as she passed behind him.

The break, when it came, came suddenly. Barry opened his eyes and asked what time it was. Lola was with him, and as she read sanity in his gaze her whole face lighted, the little lines magically faded, and she smiled that soft smile of hers.

"Ees five by the clock," she told him; then, "Oh, Bar-ree! Eet 'as been so long!"

"So long?" He seemed puzzled.

"Yes. For nearly the mont' you 'ave lay 'ere in the

Cinchbuckle, so seek, so week! Some tam we theenk you mus' die."

"A month?" His voice was wondering. "At the Cinchbuckle? Where's Barbara?"

The light went out of her eyes, the animation left her face, the little lines came back intensified. She got to her feet.

"I weel sen' her." Lola's voice sounded suddenly dead.

"But—Lola!"

In an instant she was smiling again. "We weel talk later, you an' me. Now I mus' run and tell Barbara. She weel be so glad to know you are get well."

She met Barbara and Nip hurrying along the hall. Perhaps they had heard his voice. Lola smiled brightly and her dark eyes glowed. "Bar-ree ees wake op! He ees ask for you; go to heem."

For an instant Barbara's face went white; then with a little cry she sped past the girl to Barry's room. Lola looked up at Nip, and Nip looked down at Lola. In that instant the cowboy knew infinite torture. He saw the smile fade, saw the bright eyes cloud; then she was sobbing convulsively, the tears streaming down her cheeks.

"Oh, Neep!" she cried brokenly, and swayed towards him.

The big cowboy caught her, held her gently as one would hold a child. When he spoke his voice was husky.

"Don't cry, honey. Mustn't let them hear you. Come and lie down. Poor kid, you're worn to a frazzle." He led her to Barbara's room and helped her to the bed.

Then he knelt on the floor beside her, smoothed the dark hair back from her brow, tried awkwardly to stay the tears he yearned to kiss away.

Barbara appeared at the doorway. "Nip! What's wrong with Lola?"

He looked up gravely. "The poor kid's broke under the strain, Barbara. You better send for the doc; she needs somethin' to put her to sleep."

The doctor arrived and shook his head worriedly. Lola was still sobbing, great dry sobs that wrung Nip's honest heart. The physician administered a sedative and ordered quiet and rest and care.

"She'll get 'em," promised Nip. "Barbara, send a man over to the Flyin' W and tell Tuck to stay there. I'm goin' to nurse Lola."

So it was that Nip put in the balance of the two months. He never left the girl for more than a couple of minutes at a time. He slept on a pallet by her bed, abruptly ordering Barbara to the spare bedroom. Lola was delirious for days, and when her mind finally cleared she was pathetically weak and thin.

When she began to recover, Barbara induced Nip to move his bed outside the room and came herself to sleep with the Mexican girl. Remembering the look she had surprised, she never tired of telling Lola how devoted Nip had been. At first this made little impression on Lola, but with the return of a measure of her strength she was able to notice how untiring was Nip in her service, how unselfish in his attempts to help her, how eager to carry out her slightest wish; and in time the dark eyes began to hold a look of wonder, the faintest of smiles came occasionally to her lips, a bit of color to her cheeks.

Meanwhile, Barbara attended to Barry's wants, a task which lessened with the passing of each day. Once definitely past the crisis he mended rapidly. In a week he was out of bed; in two, he was walking. At the beginning of the fourth week he ventured to ride, and at the end of the month announced his intention of returning to the Flying W.

He spent much time with Lola, holding her hand and talking to her while she lay on the bed and gazed up at him with those soft dark eyes which appeared abnormally large in her pinched face. For Barbara had told him how the girl had saved him and nursed him back to life. The telling was hard, but Barbara was honest and fair-minded, and the story came from her heart. She had learned to love the little Mexican girl, and to her credit be it said that Lola's past life could not prejudice her. Love had purged Lola, and Barbara, being a woman, saw and understood.

Barry did not remain long at the Flying W. His mother, despite the setback she had experienced through worry over her son's injury, steadily improved. Nip and Tuck had taken jealous care of her, letting the range work go for the time being, and the absence of Chet Lewis undoubtedly helped. After reassuring her as to his complete recovery, Barry left for the Cinch-buckle south line cabin. Here it was that Slater had held forth, and somewhere near it he was sure he would find some evidence of that valuable thing of which he was so positive Horace Moley had knowledge.

For a full week he tramped the hills around the cabin, looking for excavations, or cruised the little stream which separated the Cinchbuckle from the Slash B scanning the banks for signs of panning. He found not the slightest man-made hole or the smallest pile of dirt from a gold pan. His search led him to a little marshy depression in the middle of which was a pool of stagnant water. He sat wearily on a log and gazed absently at the green-scummed surface of the pond. Not a sign of Slater's activities had he found; could it be that his guess was a poor one after all? The place stank, and he finally got up and returned to the cabin.

He was eating his supper when Tuck entered. The cowboy was laboring under some repressed excitement, and waved aside Barry's invitation to join him in his meal.

"Sam Hodge is back," he announced tersely.

Barry shrugged and went on with his eating. "I'll bet he didn't bring Tug Groody with him."

"No; but he brung a friend of yours and of mine— Clement Dawn."

Barry raised his head to stare. "Clement Dawn!"

"Yeah. Got him locked in the calaboose right now. How in time did he find where Clement was when even Barbara didn't know? Or did she?"

"She did. I told her; but I haven't told another soul, not even you and Nip."

"It's a safe bet she told Clay, and Clay's been in Mescal with Steve Moley and his crowd on one drunk after another."

"Clay is weak, but he'd never betray his own brother."

"Huh. Well, anyhow Clem's in the jug with a murder charge hangin' over him."

Barry's appetite suddenly vanished. "I'm goin' to town."

Tuck wanted to accompany him, but Barry ordered him to the Flying W. It was dark when he reached Mescal, and he went directly to the sheriff's office.

"No, you can't see him," said Sam Hodge. "Nobody can but his lawyer—if he gits one. He's bein' held for murder."

"He'll have a lawyer, the best money can hire," Barry told him, and left for the Palace. Here the conversation dealt almost exclusively with Sam and his exploit. Jeff Hope and Harry Webb were at the bar talking for the benefit of any who might care to listen.

"That's a sample of the protection we git in this Basin," Webb declared. "Sam Hodge goes traipsin' off to Wyomin' after a boy who did the community a favor by rubbin' out a paid gunman, leavin' our range open for two months to Tug Groody and his outfit. And us thinkin' he's on a still hunt for Tug! I tell you we need a sheriff that ain't afraid to go after that jigger and run him ragged. It can be done, and Matt Billings is the man to do it."

Barry heard the muttering and saw the nods of agreement which greeted this statement. Evidently Hodge's action had not elevated him in the eyes of the citizens of Mescal Basin. Clement had never been a menace; Tug Groody was an ever present one. And election was but three days off.

Horace Moley, seated with Steve in an obscure corner, saw and heard it all. His long face did not change expression, and he sipped at his Scotch and soda thoughtfully. It was time, he decided, for the bold stroke. Tug had defied him by stealing from the Slash B; Tug had failed to remove Barry Weston; Tug knew that Horace was the prime factor behind the cattle thefts. In a word, Tug, once a valuable asset, now stood out on the balance sheet as a hugh liability.

"You hear 'em?" whispered Steve. "They'll elect Billings yet."

His father permitted himself a thin smile. "Wait for me here, Stevie," he said briefly, and left the place.

He went directly to the sheriff's office. Sam Hodge was inside, and waved his visitor to a chair beside the desk. For a short space the lawyer talked, and as he talked Sam's face brightened and a look of keen anticipation came over his face. Sam had been worrying about that coming election himself.

Half an hour later the sheriff entered the Palace. His head was erect and he could not avoid strutting a bit. A hush fell over the crowd at his appearance, and Sam took advantage of it by running his eye over the assemblage and uttering a terse order.

"Steve, git what Slash B men are in town and come to my office. Jeff, you and Harry Webb come too." He indicated several other men. "All of you git your horses and come ahumpin'. I jest got a tip on where Tug

Groody hides out. We're goin' after him and we're stay-in' until we git him."

Shortly thereafter they swept out of Mescal, twelve determined men all spoiling for a fight. Tug, by steal-ing from the Slash B, had alienated his one-time friends on that spread; Jeff Hope and Harry Webb, although skeptical, were anxious to come to grips with the out-law. And Sam Hodge had a soft and lucrative job at stake.

Barry was one of the crowd which watched their de-parture. Taking advantage of the sheriff's absence, he rode to the rear of the jail and stopped beneath a barred cell window. By raising in his stirrups he could peer through the opening. A man, stretched out on the iron cot, raised himself at Barry's soft greeting. He sprang from the bed, eager face turned towards the window.

"Barry!" They gripped hands through the grating.

"Hodge wouldn't let me see you. Just wanted to tell you that we aim to beat this case. I'll get the best lawyer I can find, and we'll take it clear to the Supreme Court if we have to."

"Barry, before God it's a frameup. Cal Garth was waitin' for me behind the Palace when I went after my horse. He stumbled into me like he was drunk, and when I pushed him away he started cussin' me. Barry, he called me somethin' no man can call me and live to brag about. We shot it out. It was an even break, and I killed him. It was your case all over—no witnesses, and him the pet of the Moleys. I had to run for it."

"You're not tellin' me anything I didn't guess be-fore, Clem. That's why I say we're goin' to beat this

case. It's all a part of a plot to cripple the Cinchbuckle."
He went on to explain what had happened in the Basin
since Clement's departure, until a sound at the far end
of the corridor warned Barry of the turnkey's approach.
With a hurried, "So long, old-timer; keep your chin
up!" he reined away.

Early the next morning he rode to the Cinchbuckle.
Barbara had heard of Clement's arrest and was, of
course, greatly disturbed.

"I don't know how they found out," she said. "I
haven't told a soul, and Clay declares he has never even
mentioned Clement's name."

"It doesn't matter now how they found out. They've
got him, and our job is to prove him innocent. How is
Lola?"

"Much better. Poor Nip hovers over her like a hen
with one chick. Barry, I believe he's in love with Lola."

"Who wouldn't love her?" asked Barry softly. "She's
all wool and a yard and a half wide. I'm goin' in to see
her."

Barbara did not accompany him, Alonzo J. Frothingham rode up shortly thereafter, and she accepted
his invitation to ride. He noticed at once that her gaiety
was forced, but attributed it to worry over her brother.

And even as they rode across the rangeland, Sheriff
Hodge and his party were riding doggedly among the
south hills, following a course which had been mapped
out for him by Horace Moley himself. They came at
last to a gully into which Sam turned. At the end of
another hour he halted them and spoke briefly.

"Accordin' to my information Tug has his camp at

the head of this gulch. You boys wait here while I ride ahead and scout. If you hear me shoot, come on the run."

He set out alone, riding cautiously; but Sam was no Indian when it came to woodcraft, and his horse was too big and heavy to handle well in the brush. Sam decided to circle the camp in an effort to find a place where he could see without being seen. Putting his horse to the gully bank, he managed to get him to the top. The going was bad, and he twisted and turned so much that he was finally seized with the uncomfortable feeling that he was lost. He pulled to a halt and took his bearings, then forged ahead once more, bearing to his right.

After a while he drew rein to listen, and detected a sound which he decided was the splash and gurgle of water. Horace had told him there was a spring near the camp; was this it? Dismounting, he drew his gun and pushed ahead through the brush. The bushes thinned, and daylight beyond a screen of foliage told of a clearing. He parted the brush and peered out. Before him, within a stone's throw, was the outlaw camp.

Sam's heart skipped a beat or two. Instead of circling the camp he had ridden right into it. He had a hasty impression of pasture and huts and corrals, of grazing animals and lounging men, then his eyes were drawn irresistibly to his left and he uttered a soft exclamation of alarm. A man lay at full length on the ground where he had evidently been drinking from the spring. He was staring directly at Sam, moisture

dripping from his heavy black beard. The man was
Tug Groody.

Had Hodge kept his head, all might have been well;
for Tug at first was under the impression that Sam had
brought a message from Moley; but Sam had no
thought save to get away from there. He turned to
run, tripped over some vines and went sprawling, and
the gun, which he had cocked, exploded with a roar.

Tug was on his feet in an instant, hand on his Colt,
peering about him like a cougar at bay. Following the
shot he heard the sound of shouts and the thunder of
hoofs as the posse answered what they thought was the
signal to charge. Tug's men were up and running for
their horses; but Tug saw that they would never be
able to make it. With a snarled oath, he ducked into
the brush.

The posse charged straight up the gully and into the
outlaw camp. Tug's men, realizing that they could not
escape, turned to shoot it out. The battle was short
and sanguinary, and when the smoke cleared five outlaws had paid with their lives for the destruction they
had wrought in the Basin.

That night an impatient crowd waited in the Palace
for news from the posse. Most of them were skeptical
of Hodge's success, averring that if he captured Tug
Groody it would be the first thing he had ever caught
besides a cold in the head. Horace Moley waited im-
perturbably. There was no doubt of the outcome in his
mind. Sam knew the exact location of the outlaw camp
and had sufficient men with him to wipe out Tug and
his whole crew.

He rubbed his hands together and sipped his Scotch complacently. Matt Billings would not realize his ambition to become sheriff this election; with the extinction of Tug Groody to his credit, Sam would be swept into office by popular acclaim.

The listeners heard the swift beat of hoofs outside, and as all turned expectantly towards the swinging doors, they parted to admit the sad-faced Jefferson Hope. Jeff appeared weary from his hard ride, and his long mustaches drooped dismally. They descended on him in a bunch.

"What news, Jeff? Where's the rest of your outfit?" asked Matt Billings.

"Take it easy, boys," said Jeff, waving them back. "The news is mostly good, and the rest of the boys are drivin' in a bunch of rustled stock we found. We ran plumb into Tug's men and wiped 'em out complete."

A shout of applause greeted this statement, and Horace Moley's teeth showed in a grin of triumph.

"Any of our boys hurt?" asked one of the crowd.

Jeff regarded him thoughtfully. "Well, I wouldn't say he was *hurt*. I said we tangled with Tug's *men* and wiped 'em out complete. That don't include Tug. He got away on Sam Hodge's horse. 'Pears like Sam and Tug met in the woods and had a little argyment and Sam stopped one of Tug's six-gun slugs. Seein' as it hit him plumb smack between the eyes, I reckon it didn't have time to hurt."

"Dead?" gasped Billings.

"Deader'n Christopher Columbus," said Jeff sadly.

CHAPTER XIII

MATT BUYS A DRINK

THE ELECTION, of course, went to Matt Billings. Three days was too short a time for even
a genius like Horace Moley to rally his bewildered fol-
lowers and put the heavy political machine back in gear.

"We'll have to get along without a sheriff," Horace
told Steve testily. "Fortunately we're within sight of
our goal, and when we've reached it we won't care who
is in office."

"We've been in sight of that goal for months," replied Steve surlily, "but it don't seem any nearer to me
now than it was at the beginnin'. When Al Frotling-
ham calls them notes he'll be lynched. Public opinion
won't stand for a deal like that after the promises he's
made to renew them. And the new sheriff is one of the
note holders. Looks to me like a lot of grief ahead."

Moley cackled. "You seem reluctant to leave things
to me, don't you, Stevie? I haven't failed you yet,
have I?"

"You failed to get Barry Weston."

"We all failed there. But we have just eliminated

two men who knew things. Tug Groody won't come back to talk, and Sam can't."

"You sure you got those ranchers hooked for enough?"

"Plenty. Matt and Jeff borrowed ten thousand each, and Harry Webb has since added another five thousand to the original five. Most of it went into improvements and the payment of accumulated debts. Bascomb has been carrying them for over two years, you know. They've all sold pretty close, and the drought and rustling has cut them to the bone. No; what stock they have left will never cover the loans. The bank will have to close them out."

"And the Cinchbuckle?"

"In the bag, my boy. Barbara borrowed seven thousand, and Clay has gambled away another three. In addition, the four thousand they got for their unmortgaged stock was—shall we say lost? in that poker game. The girl put up cattle for collateral, but Clay's notes will have to be met."

"What do you aim to do with Clement?"

"Convict him," snapped Moley harshly. "I owe that girl a little debt which I intend to pay. If, by some miracle, she should be able to raise enough to cover Clay's notes, I'll trade his life for the Cinchbuckle."

His long face had gone hard. Steve looked at him and nodded. This sire of his certainly had everything sewed up—everything but the Flying W.

"There still remains Weston."

Horace frowned. "Yes. Frankly, I'm afraid of him. He's the monkey wrench in the machinery. He broke up the rustling game, and I have a hunch he tipped Barbara off to the blackmailing. He wiggled out of your trap, and got away from Tug. He's too lucky to suit me. But he isn't bullet proof, and we should have somebody handy enough with a gun to polish him off."

"There's Cliff Bender and Doug Pell at the Palace."

"Ace's bouncers? They have no reason for quarreling with him, and we don't have Sam Hodge to cover us up any more."

"How about Ike Wetmiller?"

The lawyer's eyes narrowed calculatingly. "Not a bad selection. Ike knows about your rustling over the Slash B. Hm-m-m."

For a short space he sat hunched in his chair, brows bent, eyes fixed on the desk before him; then the frown vanished, and he straightened up and reached for pencil and paper. For several minutes he wrote slowly and painfully in an unaccustomed hand, then read the note carefully, added a post-script, and handed the paper to his son.

Dear miss Dawn, the cattle you lost were russled through the help of Ike Wetmiller. he planted them where Tug could get them and saw to it that the crew did not get wise.   a Friend
p.s. don't tell ike about this letter, he might figger out who sent it.

Steve looked up. "Well?"

"She won't keep him after that. When he is discharged he will probably come to you. You will suggest that the only one who could have informed Barbara is

Barry Weston. That ought to take care of the matter, eh?"

Steve nodded. "Address the envelope and I'll drop it in the box when nobody's lookin'."

That same day Barry brought a lawyer from Hartsville, and sent him to see Clement at once. When the lawyer rejoined Barry, he was not at all optimistic.

"The evidence is going to be difficult to get around. According to the testimony of the sheriff, now deceased, Garth's gun was found loaded and holstered. Polmateer and the two others who found him will testify to that effect also. To combat their testimony we have only Clement's story and the improbability that a gunman with Garth's reputation could have been shot directly from the front without even drawing his weapon."

"Clement didn't shoot the man without giving him a chance."

"I agree with you; but will the jury?"

Barry was considerably disturbed as he rode to the Cinchbuckle. Clement was in a tight spot and his flight seemed to emphasize his guilt. A thought occurred to Barry on the way out, and after briefly telling Barbara of the lawyer's arrival, he left her to pay Lola a visit.

Nip was seated by the girl's bed and got up at Barry's entrance, but Weston waved him back into the chair.

"Just dropped in for a minute," he said, and inquired of the girl how she felt. Lola was rapidly improving, and Barry shrewdly guessed it was due in no small measure to the attention and untiring efforts of Nip.

"Lola, I want to ask you a question," he said at last.

"Clement is in a bad spot, and about the only way to save him is to prove that somebody reloaded Garth's gun and put it back into his holster. Do you know anything about it? Has anybody ever hinted such a thing to you?"

She regarded him solemnly. "Bar-ree, I would tell eef I know, but I don'. Ees Steve you theenk might tell me, no?"

Barry was embarrassed. "Well—anybody that was in it; Steve, or Ace, or his two bouncers."

"I'm not know," she said sadly. "I weesh I do. Barbara ees treat me lak I'm her seester. I would lak to 'elp her so moch."

He changed the conversation immediately, and soon after left them. When he went out to the gallery it was to find Alonzo J. Frothingham. The banker greeted him pleasantly.

"Just killing time while Miss Dawn gets into her riding togs," he explained. "Sit down, won't you?"

Barry did not feel much like lingering, but he reluctantly seated himself, and for several minutes they discussed cattle and the range.

"Everybody is making improvements but you," said Frothingham. "Glad to see it. You certainly ought to join the procession, Weston. I'd be more than happy to finance any expansion you might plan. After all—"

"I know," smiled Barry. "My prosperity is yours."

Frothingham laughed. "You've heard it before, eh? Well, it's true. A progressive banker should work hand in hand with his clients. Think it over; a few thousands would do wonders for the Flying W."

Barbara came out on the gallery, and they both got to their feet. She was frowning over a sheet of note paper. Without a word she handed it to Barry.

He read the anonymous letter quietly, then handed it back. "What are you goin' to do?"

"Discharge him. I asked Lola about it and she confirmed the letter. Steve had mentioned the matter to her. Barry, you were right. I suppose I was blind."

"Just loyal, Barbara. You won't give away Lola?"

"It won't be necessary. I'll give Wetmiller his time and tell him to go."

Ike Wetmiller and the crew were working near the bunkhouse, getting equipment ready for the roundup. Barry saw her call him aside and speak to him. He replied, waving his hands as he protested; but she turned away and came back to the house. For a moment he stared after her, then, with an oath, flung the harness he had been mending to the ground and went after his belongings. When he rode to the house Barbara was waiting for him with a check. He took it from her, flashed a malignant look at Barry, and sullenly rode away.

"Don't let me keep you from your ride," said Barry. "I'll go in and talk with Lola and Nip." They rode away together, chatting animatedly, Barbara apparently having forgotten Barry as soon as she was mounted. His face tightened. He had come to understand men, but the ways of women were as unfathomable as the deepest sea.

He did not linger long at the Cinchbuckle. A feeling of depression had seized him and he was in a dangerous mood when he entered Mescal. Matt Billings hailed him from the sheriff's office, and what that officer had to say did not improve matters.

"Ike Wetmiller's down at the Palace lappin' up some Dutch courage. Miss Dawn fired him, and for some reason he's blamin' you. What's the trouble?"

Barry told him about the rustling he had witnessed and the letter which accused Wetmiller. "Somebody on the Cinchbuckle was helpin' those rustlers, and it must have been Ike. They got wise to my bein' in the rustlin' crew, and turned the cattle loose before I could bring witnesses to see them in the corral. Likely Ike thinks I told Barbara he was in the deal."

"You want me to lock him up?"

"No. If he's goin' to make anything of it, lockin' him up will only postpone the issue. Let him turn his wolf loose if he feels lucky. I'm gettin' sick of this underhand work."

"He's mighty slick with a six, Barry. Mebbe you'd better steer clear of him until he sobers up."

"I'm not runnin' from a sneakin' cattle thief."

"All right, son; but don't you take no chances."

Barry nodded and turned away. He had come to town to order supplies for the Flying W, and so went directly to the store. As he entered, he noticed a lounger leaving, and felt sure the fellow was carrying the news of his whereabouts to the Palace. Bascomb waited on him nervously, evidently well aware of the trap into which he was expected to walk.

He went outside and stood for a moment rolling a cigarette. The sun was low, but there was still light enough to see by. Down the street a man sat on the edge of the watering trough outside the Palace. There was nobody else in sight except Matt Billings, who was walking down the sidewalk on the other side of the street. Barry turned towards the Palace, and before he had covered fifty feet the man on the trough got up, stretched, and sauntered through the swinging doors into the saloon.

At the corner of the Palace, Barry turned left and followed the passageway to the alley. The rear door was locked, but the window he had broken had been repaired with a sheet of cardboard which he quickly cut away with his knife. Unfastening the sash, he raised it and slipped over the sill. The room was empty and in semi-darkness. He crossed to the door which led into the saloon and turned the knob. As he slowly opened the door the sound of suppressed voices reached him. There was a tenseness in the atmosphere of the place which subtly enveloped him as he stepped to the dance platform and stood looking down the long room.

He spotted Wetmiller at once. Ike stood at Barry's end of the bar, half turned to face the front door. The rest of the patrons had left the bar, carrying their drinks to tables well out of the expected lane of fire. Ace Polmateer stood behind the short length of bar which extended to the wall. He, too, was watching the front door. Two bartenders mechanically polished glasses, ready to duck to safety; and seated in chairs at the very edge of the dancing platform, their backs to Barry, were the two gunmen bouncers, Cliff Bender and Doug Pell.

It was so quiet that Barry distinctly heard the thud of bootheels on the plank walk outside. A wave of suppressed excitement swept the room like the static electricity which precedes a lightning bolt. All eyes were turned to the swinging doors, hands gripped table or glass, jaw muscles tightened. Wetmiller flashed a quick glance over his shoulder towards the two gunmen, received a slight nod of assurance, and jerked his head to the front as the doors parted.

Sheriff Matt Billings ste ped into the room.

A sigh of escaped breath like the rustling of wind in autumn leaves broke the silence; the frigid attitudes of expectancy were relaxed; feet shuffled on the hard floor.

Matt spoke drawlingly. "Kinda quiet, boys. How about a drink?"

His gaze passed slowly along the faces which lined the side wall. Men shook their heads or held up glasses to show they were already occupied.

Matt grinned slightly. "Must be tired, settin' around this way. I see Ike Wetmiller is on his feet. Have a drink, Ike."

"Not drinkin' now," Wetmiller replied tightly. "I'm waitin' for somebody. He was just seen comin' down the street. Didn't talk him out of comin' in, did you, Matt?"

"Why, no. I expect he'll be along. After all, I don't feel much like drinkin' myself. I'll set down too." He selected a chair where he could watch the bouncers. "Sure you ain't bitin' off more'n you can chaw, Ike?"

Wetmiller swore. "If you're tryin' to get my goat,

Matt, your luck ain't very good. I'll show you how my digestion is when that lousy son walks in."

A voice spoke behind him. "Don't happen to be talkin' of me, do you, Ike?"

Even in that tense moment Barry was able to appreciate the consternation which followed his words. As though attached to the same string, faces along the wall swung in a half circle from the front door to where he stood in the shadows of the dance floor. He had the impression of a thousand round eyes staring at him. Ike stiffened as though pricked by a pin; the two gunmen started so plainly that he easily observed their spasmodic movement. He spoke quietly, almost drawlingly.

"The two Palace peacemakers will remain seated durin' the performance. Turn around, Ike."

Wetmiller, rigid and erect, turned slowly. His hands were held away from his body as though to demonstrate that he had no intention of drawing as he faced about. For a moment the two men faced each other, Ike a bit white-lipped as he realized that the advantage he expected to hold was lost to him. Barry stood easily, arms folded. As invariably happened in moments of emergency, he was cool and entirely clear-minded.

"Heard you were lookin' for me, Ike. In my language that means only one thing. Start explainin' right quick or go for your gun."

There was no way out of it for Ike. He could have denied that he meant Barry any harm, but to do so would be to sacrifice any respect folks might have for him. Not for a moment did he hesitate."

"You're danged tootin' I am, you lousy son!" he spat, and went for his gun.

Fast he was; unbelievably fast. Not for nothing was that tied-down holster carried so low on his thigh. Hand and gun were but blurs of motion, and he got in his shot fully half a second before Barry; and half a second between experienced gunmen is a very long interval.

Barry, watching keenly, took one step to his right as he drew. Just one step, but that was sufficient to cause Ike to miss. Barry felt a tug at his coat as the bullet passed between his side and his arm. He fired quickly, aiming at Wetmiller's broad shoulder.

Ike spun around, tangled his feet, and piled on the floor. His gun flew from his lax fingers, but like a wounded wolf he squirmed around and clutched the weapon with his left hand. Barry aimed deliberately and fired, and the gun was torn from Wetmiller's clutch and sent skittering along the floor.

Matt Billings recovered it. Ike had fallen on his face, unable to support himself with either arm.

"Show's over," announced Matt calmly. "Ike *did* bite off more'n he could chaw. Cliff, you and Doug take him over to the doc's. The rest of you boys belly up; we're goin' to have that drink now."

CHAPTER XIV

THE JAWS CLOSE

ALONZO J. FROTHINGHAM was graver than usual when he stepped from his horse before the Cinchbuckle ranch house. The zero hour had arrived and he found himself the victim of conflicting emotions. Never before had a girl stirred him as had Barbara Dawn; he had reached the point where he carried the memory of her face with him through his waking hours and dreamed of her at night.

Lola was on the gallery, reclining listlessly in a big chair which the ever attentive Nip had arranged for her. He attempted to shake the feeling of depression which had gripped him by greeting her lightly, but Lola answered shortly and closed her eyes again. She did not like Alonzo J.

"Barbara weel be 'ere soon, She ees expec' you."

He seated himself on the edge of the veranda, swinging his quirt idly. A horseman was approaching from the direction of the Flying W, and presently he recognized Barry Weston. A frown puckered his brow; the hunch persisted that Barbara, despite her apparent indifference, loved this man, and the knowledge piqued him. He was his old complacent self, however, when Barry swung from his horse and came up on the veranda.

"I seem always to pick a time for visitin' when you and Barbara are goin' ridin'," said Weston. Neither words nor actions betrayed the annoyance he felt. He had come over determined to pay his court to Barbara, to strive to win back the place in her affections he at one time held. In Frothingham he instintively recognized a dangerous rival; the man was cultured and suave and handsome, and possessed of a captivating air which invariably drew one to him.

"It does seem to happen that way, doesn't it? We must get together and work out a schedule which won't conflict. Ah! Here you are, Miss Dawn. Shall we ride? Or would you rather chat with your visitor?"

Barbara answered indifferently. "Barry's an old friend; he will be dropping in again. Besides," she smilingly added, "I have a suspicion that he really came over to talk with Lola."

The Mexican girl stiffened. "Barbara, you are mak fon!"

"Of course, dear; but you will entertain him while I'm gone, won't you?" She ran lightly down the steps and permitted Frothingham to help her into the saddle. Barry watched them as they rode away, his face inscrutable.

Lola spoke quietly. "Barbara is get ver' 'elpless, no? She mus' 'ave somebody to leeft her on the *caballo*."

Barry turned to her. "You girls got me beat. Barbara

can mount and dismount four times while Frothingham is huntin' for the stirrup."

"For one who on'erstan' us our ways are easy to read. . . . Bar-ree, you lof her ver' moch, no?"

He regarded her quietly. "Very much, Lola."

Her features contracted slightly and she leaned back in the chair. "Ees so plain to see," she said. Barry never knew the effort her next words cost. "She ees lof you too."

"Lola!" In an instant he was standing over her, tense, exultant, his direct gaze burning into hers.

She smiled wanly. "Ees so. Ah, you men are so stupid! Why you theenk she ees act so col' to you? Why ees she let these other man 'elp her on the *caballo?* Why ees she laff an' seem so 'appy?"

"Why—why because she enjoys bein' with him, I reckon."

"But no! Oh, my frien', you 'ave moch to learn. Eef she care for these man you theenk she would show heem so plain? We women are not lak that; some tam we 'urt the one we lof mos'. Ees w'en she ees not know we watch that we mus' look. I see her stan' at the window, her face so sad and weeth the dream in her eyes. Of who ees she theenk? Not of these man, for she ees not look towards Mescal; she ees look towards the Flying W."

He dropped to one knee beside her and his eager hand found her small lax one and covered it. "Lola," he said earnestly, "you are the best buddy a fella ever had!"

For a long moment Lola's soft eyes met his burning

ones, and, had he been less occupied with thoughts of another, he might have read the secret they could not hide. She smiled slowly. "Ah, yes; Lola ees the good frien', no? But get to your feet, Bar-ree, for they are come back."

He got up quickly, painfully aware that his position was not that of a mere friend. Barbara and Frothingham were riding towards the house, and so intent had he been on Lola's words that he had not heard the soft thud of hoofs on the grass. He stood awkward and uncomfortable as Barbara swung from her horse and ran up the steps. She smiled very sweetly.

"Just forgot my quirt. I must be getting old."

When they had gone again, Barry seated himself disconsolately on the edge of the gallery. Lola watched him beneath lowered lashes, and presently laughed.

"The goose, she ees cook', no?"

"Lola, I reckon it is," he answered dolefully.

"Ees good. Mees Barbara weel 'ave somet'ing to theenk about."

Barbara, in the meanwhile, rode quietly beside Frothingham, listening to his bright sallies without really hearing them. A feeling of utter misery filled her. Barry loved Lola; his position at her side, the very intentness of the gaze he bent upon her, could have no other interpretation. She caught Frothingham's comment:

"Barry seems to be quite enamored of our Mexican *señorita*, doesn't he?"

She replied quietly. "He has every reason to be; she

saved his life. And Lola is a sweet girl; I've come to love her very much."

He shrugged. "But a dance-hall girl, Barbara! Surely he could have made a better choice than that."

She did not answer, but unknowingly Alonzo J. Frothingham had erected a barrier between them that he would never be able to batter down. Barbara was loyal to the soul of her; the little Mexican girl had won her completely, and she had come to know that beneath the hard shell with which a careless life had necessarily surrounded her was a heart of virgin gold.

For a while they rode in silence, reaching at last a clump of live oaks at the edge of the south road. Here they drew rein and sat their horses in the cool shade.

"Barbara," he said suddenly, "I've something to say to you."

Instinctively she sensed what was coming, but saw no way to avoid it.

He went on tensely. "I have reached a cross-road in my life, and it is in the hands of Fate as to which way I turn. I have always believed that I possess great capacity for either good or evil. You must judge for yourself as to the direction I have exerted that capacity; but regardless of what I am now I feel that with the proper woman at my side to guide and direct and advise, I could reach the heights. Barbara, I love you, and I want you to marry me."

He had chosen his words carefully so as to tell her neither too much nor too little. To give him his due, he had honestly convinced himself that if she accepted his proposal he would ditch Horace Moley and his crooked schemes and strive to bend his talents towards a lawful career.

At her impatient movement he urged his horse closer to her and continued before she could speak. "I've worked hard at the bank, and I'm ready for a holiday. I want you to share it. Let it be our honeymoon—one that we could never forget. Think of it, Barbara! The sunny skies of Mexico—the soft moon—the twang of guitars! It would be a dream come true. And afterwards we could live in the East, in the city, where you could see something else besides the eternal hills and the dusty rangeland. Theatres, parties, dances! Dear, say you'll share it with me; say you'll marry me."

He reached out to grasp her hand, but she kneed her horse away and at a safe distance shook her head at him.

"No. No, it isn't possible. It all sounds awfully nice, and I wouldn't be honest if I didn't admit that I'd like to visit the big cities and go to the theatres and parties and dances. But after all I was born near the eternal hills and dusty rangeland, and I love them. And I don't love you, Al. I dislike to hurt you, but I don't love you."

For a moment he sat looking at her, a pained expression on his face; then she saw his eyes harden, saw the muscles of his jaws bulge.

"So it's this Weston fellow after all!"

Barbara did not answer, but she knew now for a certainty what she had suspected in the past: that beneath the veneer of good nature and gentility which clothed the man was a core of selfishness and egotism and vindictiveness.

They rode back to the ranch in silence, and he immediately took his departure. His vanity had been wounded, and he now felt a hot resentment toward this girl he had professed to love and the tall, somber Barry Weston who, he felt sure, had succeeded where he had failed. He was in an excellent mood for what was ahead of him. He had left the decision to Fate, and Fate had given him the answer.

It was noon of the next day when the bank clerk called at Horace Moley's office. He appeared worried.

"Sorry to bother you, Mr. Moley, but I can't locate Mr. Frothingham. I inquired at the hotel, but nobody has seen him since supper last night. I thought you might know where I could find him."

"Probably at the Cinchbuckle," said Moley. "Go right on with your work. If you run short of cash, let me know. I have the combination to the vault."

The man was back shortly before closing time. "I'm afraid I'll have to trouble you to open the vault," he said respectfully. "I must have some more cash to honor a check of Mr. Hope's."

Moley accompanied him to the bank to find Jeff Hope waiting on the sidewalk. The lawyer explained. "Sorry to keep you waiting, Jeff, but Mr. Frothingham isn't about and I am the only other one who knows the combination to the vault."

Hope was surprised. "Didn't know you was connected with the bank," he said as they went inside.

"My dear man," Horace told him blandly, "now that

the institution is on a firm basis I don't mind telling you that I own it."

Jeff was still pondering over this when Moley drew open the big door and stood for a moment gazing at the interior of the vault. Suddenly he bent forward and started fumbling among some papers, evidently searching for something; then he straightened and turned to the clerk, and Jeff saw that his face was tight.

"Are you quite certain that the currency isn't in the little safe?" he asked, and at the tone of his voice the man started.

"Quite certain, sir. We keep only enough for current needs there."

"Go out and find Sheriff Billings at once and send him to me. And keep your mouth shut."

Jeff Hope was staring. "You mean—you mean Frothingham's—skipped?"

Moley leaned against the counter and passed his hand over his forehead. He appeared stunned—broken.

"I—I—Jeff, it looks like it. If he has, I'm a ruined man."

Jeff almost flew from the bank to spread the news. A crowd soon gathered about the entrance, which by this time was closed and locked. Through the milling citizens of Mescal Matt Billings forced his way. The door was opened at his knock and he slipped through to face a pale and tight-lipped Moley.

"What is it, Horace? What's this they're sayin' outside?"

"Matt, I'm ruined—ruined! Frothingham has taken every cent of currency and all the negotiable bonds in the vault. I backed him from the start—thought him the soul of honesty, and he betrayed me! Get after him. Bring him back. A thousand dollars to you if you do! Make it five thousand! Get out posters—notify the adjoining counties—but bring him back. I tell you I'm ruined!"

Matt departed on the run, but there was nothing at first to tell him in which direction to search for the missing cashier. He had just come from the hotel after questioning the help, when a man rode into town with Frothingham's horse on a lead rope.

"Found him grazin' by the road when I was comin' to town," explained the fellow. "Ten miles north of Mescal on the stage road."

Within five minutes Matt and a hastily summoned posse rode out of town at a furious gallop, headed north. And hardly had they departed when a pasty-faced clerk slipped through the doorway of the bank and hurriedly tacked up a penciled notice:

This bank will be closed until further notice.
Horace Moley, Prop.

The wolf had closed his jaws!

CHAPTER XV

THE WOLF SNARLS

THERE WAS consternation in the Basin that day. The news spread like a prairie fire, and before the day was over had carried to the farthest reaches of the range. Frothingham had been well liked; his frank, easy manner and apparent sympathy for the ranchers had won their confidence; to have him suddenly branded a thief stunned them.

When they finally reconciled themselves to this unexpected situation the shadow of Horace Moley rose to confront them. His ownership of the bank had been kept a careful secret; even Steve had been unaware of it until his father had seen fit to make the news public. The lawyer talked freely now, and his denunciation of Alonzo J. Frothingham was bitter. The man had come to him a year before armed with credentials of the very best. Moley now believed them forged. He had suggested a partnership, Moley to furnish the capital, he the banking experience and executive ability. Horace had agreed, but, knowing that folks in the Basin were prejudiced against him, had insisted that his connection with the institution be kept secret.

The bank prospered and to all appearances Frothingham was the soul of integrity. He, Horace Moley, had been cleverly duped. At first a bit cautious, he had furnished capital sufficient only to keep the bank going; later his confidence in Frothingham grew to such an extent that he had entrusted practically all his cash and securities to the banker's keeping. Now Frothingham had absconded and he, Horace Moley, was ruined. Except for the building and a few investments and balances in other banks, nothing remained but notes receivable. These, of course, would be called immediately. So said Horace Moley.

This last statement proved the crowning blow to the Basin ranchers. The notes were demand ones, secured by airtight mortgages on their property. To pay them would be impossible; the fact that the makers had been promised the privilege of renewing them at will would not hold for a minute, the one who had made the promise being a thief and a scoundrel. Moley, when Jeff Hope spoke to him on the subject, disclaimed any knowledge of the bargain; even said that Frothingham had no authority to lend his money under such conditions. The notes would have to be paid immediately or foreclosure steps would be taken at once. Court would be in session within a few days, and judgment would be secured. The lawyer was adamant; they must pay or turn their property over to him.

Jeff Hope and Harry Webb talked the matter over outside Moley's office.

"I reckon there ain't no use fightin'," sighed Jeff. "He can git judgment all right, and I sure can't satisfy it. Even if we got a fair price for the spreads, which ain't noways likely at a sheriff's sale, what we get over and above the judgment would be et up by lawyer's fees and such like. No, Harry, I reckon I'll turn her over, lock, stock, and bar'l, and pull out."

"Me, too," said Webb grimly. "I was fixin' to git out a long time ago, but Frothingham talked me outa it. Jerry Weston's gone, and so are Charley Dawn and George Brent. This'll bust Matt Billings too, but he's got the sheriff's job to keep him goin'. Let Horace take the danged spread if he wants it; I'll find me a bit of new range over in Arizona and start over."

The most miserable person in the Basin at that moment was Clay Dawn. The news of Frothingham's defalcation had come to him like a thunder clap. Save for a few dollars he had gambled away three thousand, always in the hope of winning back the four he had originally lost. Seven thousand dollars had slipped through his fingers within the short space of three months! This, added to the seven thousand Barbara had borrowed, would ruin the Cinchbuckle. Their stock, depleted by drought and disease and rustling, would possibly bring enough to cover Barbara's notes; but the three thousand he had borrowed would have to be paid, and since he had borrowed it for the purpose of improving the Cinchbuckle, the money had become a loan against the property rather than a personal one.

Until late in the night he sat in the Palace drinking steadily, moody, silent, dangerous. Steve and his friends from the Slash B wisely kept away from him. Stupid with drink, the last of his money gone, he staggered to the hotel stable and slept in the hay. When he awoke the next morning he saddled up and rode back into the hills, and for several hours sat in silence fighting it out with himself.

His first impulse was to leave the Basin. He had disgraced his sister and betrayed her trust. He did not blame Steve, although it had occurred to him that Moley won with surprizing consistency. In the end he rejected the idea of flight. That would leave Barbara alone to face the calamity. Clay was young and by nature weak of will; but he was no quitter. In that moment some of the courage which he had inherited from his father manifested itself. He finally rode to the Flying W.

Barry was out on the range, but Clay found him and led him to a shady spot on the slope of the north hills. Here he told Weston everything, speaking deliberately and not sparing himself one whit.

Barry heard him through in silence, troubled gaze on the rolling Basin rangeland. When Clay had finished, he remained for a moment without speaking. The boy's manly confession had touched him, and when he finally turned to Clay his eyes reflected the respect he felt.

"Runnin' away from trouble never pays in the end. I caused my mother five years of heartache because I got scared and ran. Clement had the deck stacked against him by runnin'. Had he stayed right there with Cal Garth's body until the sheriff arrived, there would have been no reloadin' of Cal's gun. I reckon when you get right down to it you've shown more real guts than either Clem or myself will ever have. Go straight to Barbara and tell her about it just like you told me. She's a soldier; she'll stand by you. And she'll be proud of you even while she's scoldin' you."

Clay's eyes were moist. "Thanks, Barry. I'll do it, but only one one condition." He eyed Barry directly, almost fiercely. "If I ever touch another card or take another drink of liquor, I want you to bull-whip the hide clean off me."

Barry thumped him on the back. "Clay, I sure promise; but I'm bettin' it's one promise I'll never have to keep."

Clay's fine young body showed determination in every line. "I want to ask one more favor. Barbara thinks a heap of you. I'd sort of like you to ride over to the spread in an hour or so. It's goin' to hit her hard, comin' like it has on top of Clem's trouble, and maybe you can cheer her up a bit."

"Clay, I'll sure do it. I'll start in an hour."

That session of Barbara's and Clay's must forever be a secret locked in the hearts of both of them; neither ever mentioned the matter thereafter. But that day marked the beginning of an understanding of each other that had never existed before; an understanding and sympathy which they were to carry through life. And on that day Clay became a man.

When Barry found them they were seated on the gallery quietly talking. Barbara's eyes were shining, although he thought he could detect the trace of tears. He greeted them casually and dropped into a chair.

"Well," he said, "what are we goin' to do about it?"

Barbara answered. "Barry, I don't know. Those notes will be called, and of course we can't meet them in full. I am going to Horace Moley; perhaps if I pay him half he can be persuaded to take a new note for the balance."

"I'm afraid it won't work," said Clay. "Barbara has been tellin' me just why you think Moley wants the Cinchbuckle. She also told me about the rustlin' and the blackmailin'. She didn't tell me before, and I don't blame her. I been stayin' in Mescal most of the time, and in addition to that I just wasn't worthy of bein' told." His face wore a flush of shame, but he went on steadily. "If it is true that Horace Moley wants this spread, the opportunity he's been waitin' for is his. He's a wolf, and when he once gets somethin' in his jaws he won't let go."

"We can try," said Barbara bravely. "I'm afraid I hurt my chances by talking to him the way I did when I discovered he was blackmailing us, but I'm ready to eat any kind of humble pie if it will save the Cinchbuckle."

Clay was pessimistic. "Now that my eyes are open, I can see a little farther than the end of my nose. What a fool I've been! I was robbed of that four thousand dollars. It was part of the plan, just like the rustlin' of our breeders. You notice it was *breeders* we lost—the foundation of our herd. The whole thing was planned to weaken us so Horace could get the spread."

"When you speak of the Devil," said Barry, "he generally pops up. Here comes Horace's buggy now. I reckon we'd better leave him alone with Barbara. Let's go in and visit with Lola and Nip."

"They've gone for a ride, Barry," Barbara told him. "Lola has been improving wonderfully; she's almost herself again."

Barry and Clay led their horses to the back of the house before Moley was close enough to identify them. They waited the outcome in the bunkhouse, talking quietly.

When Horace Moley drew up before the gallery, Barbara was standing at the steps awaiting him. He tied quickly and came up to the veranda, his long face hard, his eyes cold. He greeted her stiffly, took the chair she indicated, and sat there with his beaver hat balanced on his skinny knees.

"I assume that you can guess the object of my call, Miss Dawn," he said. "It's about those notes of yours. Demand notes, if you will remember. I would like to reach an understanding with regard to them."

Barbara's face brightened a little. A compromise of some kind, it seemed, might be possible after all.

"I'm glad you called," she said. "We are horribly worried, of course. You must have suffered a great loss through Mr. Frothingham's breach of faith."

"It was cold-blooded robbery," grated Horace. "The man is a thief. I have been utterly ruined by the scoundrel. Friend of yours, wasn't he?"

"He was." She colored slightly. "We were all deceived by him."

"About these notes. I must recover, and recover quickly. They represent assets of the bank; we must reach some understanding immediately."

"Mr. Moley, I shall be more than glad to meet you half way."

"No half way about it," snapped the lawyer. "Young lady, I hold notes of yours totaling seven thousand dollars, and notes of your brother amounting to three thousand more. They are all binding on the partnership. Are you prepared to pay me ten thousand dollars with interest to date."

"Why—why, no, Mr. Moley, we are not. I had hoped—"

"No use to hope. It was my hard-earned money that Frothingham squandered in this Basin. I did not know he was scattering it broadcast; he must have had a queer streak of generosity that permitted him to share it with his friends. I intend to recover every cent."

"Of course. And we can pay you in time. I believe I could manage to raise half of it in thirty days; I could surely get the rest within a year."

"A year! Do you think me crazy? Impossible to consider such a proposition, Miss Dawn."

"I thought you mentioned something about an understanding, Mr. Moley."

"Only as regards the manner in which the notes are to be met. The question of time does not enter into it. The notes have been called; I have mailed you a written demand. Failure to meet them means that I must start proceedings against you and your brother. I shall certainly secure judgment, and the ranch will be sold to the highest bidder. In that event you will have to bear the cost of the proceedings. I'm afraid there will be little left. Harry Webb and Jeff Hope saw this at once, and have agreed to save trouble by deeding their ranches to me at once. I believe it would be to your interest to do likewise."

"I couldn't do that," said Barbara firmly, "without first exhausting every means to raise the money."

Horace was annoyed. The Cinchbuckle was the key ranch, and he must have it at any cost. Like Steve, he was finding it increasingly hard to curb his cupidity.

"At what amount do you value the ranch?" he asked. "Leave sentiment out of it, please. Just assume that it is being sold by the sheriff. What amount is it likely to bring?"

"In its present condition, possibly ten thousand dollars," she replied bitterly.

"Just enough to liquidate the notes. In addition there would be interest and costs. Miss Dawn, to expedite the matter and settle it amicably and quickly I will pay you two thousand dollars and cancel the notes in exchange for a deed to the property."

She shook her head stubbornly. "As long as there is a chance remaining I must refuse."

"You're crazy," he told her shortly. "What chance have you? Where are you going to pick up ten thousand dollars? And then there is the matter of Clement. His trial comes up soon. Accommodate me in this matter and I will defend him myself, free of charge, and win his freedom for you."

"Just what do you mean by that? What could you

do, in the face of the evidence, that another can not do?"

He leered at her. "There are ways that you know nothing of. I have the reputation of being a shrewd lawyer. I am acquainted with the witnesses and I am not without influence. They may have been—mistaken."

For a long moment she stared at him. Almost had he admitted what she already believed—that the whole thing had been a frame-up. The man before her was utterly vile; she could no more trust his promises than she could make herself a party to his crookedness. Her head went up.

"Clement is innocent. We will have him acquitted in the regular way. As to the ranch, something may turn up to save it for us."

"Perhaps. Manna once fell from Heaven, I believe."

He left in a huff, whipping his horse into a run. The girl's stubbornness irked him beyond measure; certainly it seemed that a malign Fate was taking a fiendish pleasure in frustrating him.

Barry and Clay joined her on the gallery, and heard her story through without interruption.

"It's like I said," Clay declared moodily. "The old lobo wants the ranch and wants it badly. And I don't know what we can do about it."

"If they would only catch Frothingham," she said desperately. "If the money were recovered we might get an extension."

"Don't you believe it. The notes remain demand

notes regardless of whether or not the money is recovered. It wouldn't help us a bit."

Barry spoke thoughtfully. "Barbara mentioned one thing that Moley said that struck me. It was about Frothingham's generosity in sharin' the money of the bank with the Basin ranchers. It seems to me that if I was plannin' to run off with my bank's cash I wouldn't go around lendin' thirty or forty thousand dollars right before I checked out."

"Maybe he had to leave in a hurry," suggested Clay. "He must have been a crook; maybe he thought they were about to catch up with him."

"And maybe," added Barry quietly, "his abscondin' was a part of Horace Moley's scheme."

Clay jerked erect. "You mean Horace knew all about it?"

"The plot—if there is one—isn't against the Cinchbuckle alone. The night I came home I caught my stepfather and Steve Moley in the act of forgin' a deed to the Flyin' W. They want that spread too. A year ago George Brent was sold out—through the bank. Harry Webb and Jeff Hope have deeded their spreads over to Moley, and likely Matt Billings will have to do the same. If Moley wants to gain control of Mescal Basin, he couldn't have planned a better way of gettin' it than by havin' Frothingham lend the ranchers plenty of money and then skip out so that the notes could be called."

"Barry, that's an awful far-fetched theory; but it covers everything!"

"It's just a guess, and we haven't a bit of proof.

That's been the trouble all along—no witnesses. Nobody saw the rustlin' but me; nobody knew about Barbara's givin' Moley the money; nobody knew that he owned the bank; even you couldn't take the stand and swear that you were robbed of your money. Moley is a lawyer, and a sharp one. He's covered up all around. We can believe all we want and even *know* certain things to be true; but we haven't a single witness to back us up, and if we made any accusations we'd just be openin' ourselves to a libel suit."

They were moodily discussing this when a horseman rode into the yard. It was one of the crew with the mail and the latest news from town. Matt Billings had returned with his posse. Not a sign of Frothingham had they found; nobody had seen the missing cashier, nor had he left a single clue except the abandoned horse. And Matt, too, had deeded his ranch to Horace Moley.

When the man had ridden away, Barry got to his feet.

"I'm goin' after Frothingham myself. The more I think of it the more convinced I am that Moley is behind this just as he has been behind everything else. If I can nail Frothingham I'll squeeze the truth out of him."

"Where are you goin' to look for him?"

"If you were an abscondin' cashier, which way would you head?"

"South," said Clay after a moment. "Plumb across the Border."

"And if you wanted to throw folks off your trail,

you might manage to leave your horse on the stage road leadin' north."

"By jacks, I would! Have two horses, and head south with the other!"

Barbara's eyes were shining. "Barry, I believe you've hit it! I remember now something Frothingham said the last time I rode with him. It was about a vacation under the sunny skies of Mexico." She colored slightly at the memory.

"I'm goin' with you," announced Clay.

"Glad to have you. We'll take Nip and Tuck. . . . Here come Nip and Lola now."

Nip and the Mexican girl trotted their horses to the rack and swung to the ground. Barry noticed that the roses were again in Lola's cheeks, and that Nip appeared in good spirits. They came up on the gallery and the whole story was retold for their benefit.

"I'm ready to go," announced Nip. "My patient done got well in spite of her nurse. But what about Tuck? We sure ain't goin' to leave your ma alone."

Lola spoke quietly. "I weel stay weeth 'er. Me, I'm good cook. I weel tak good care of Bar-ree's *madre*."

That same evening four determined riders took the trail which led over the south hills and into Mexico.

CHAPTER XVI

THE WAGES OF SIN

THE EVENING of the third day they crossed the Rio Grande and succeeded in getting supper and a poorly ventilated room in the village of Torres. Here they had hoped to secure some information regarding the missing cashier, but their inquiries were answered with shrugs and the shaking of heads.

"He'll hardly stop for any length of time until he reaches a large town where he can lose himself in the shuffle," said Barry. "The question is, did he follow the river east or west, or did he keep on into the interior?"

Clay answered thoughtfully. "He might have gone east hopin' to reach a seaport where he could get a ship for Europe."

"Sure," agreed Nip. "Also he might have gone west knowin' that folks would figger he went east."

They decided finally to follow the river towards the east until they were certain Frothingham had not traveled that way, then search to the west. If they were unsuccessful in both directions, they would head for the interior.

They started the next morning, riding swiftly along the Border, stopping at every hovel and town on the road. No one had seen Frothingham; there was no evidence that he had passed that way. Still they pressed on, camping in the open at night, picking up what supplies they needed and could comfortably carry in the towns or at the occasional *ranchos* they encountered. Four days of this convinced them that they were on the wrong track, so they retraced their steps and followed the Border westward.

They had no better luck. Doggedly they returned to their starting point and headed by the best road into the interior. And just when they were about to give up the chase as hopeless, they picked up information which sent their hopes soaring.

It was the end of the twentieth day after leaving the Flying W, and they were tired and disheartened and painfully aware that affairs in the Basin must be approaching their final climax. They entered a town at sunset and stopped at the nearest *cantina*.

"I reckon we're licked," Barry told them grimly. "Frothingham must have gone north after all. We'll bed down here and start back tomorrow."

They turned their horses over to a Mexican boy and went into the saloon. Lining up at the bar they ordered drinks, and once again, almost mechanically, Barry inquired about a tall, well-dressed American traveling alone.

The bartender's face lighted. "But of a surety, *señor*, one such passed through here."

"He did?" came in a chorus of four voices. Their weariness was gone like mist before the sun.

"*Si, señors.* One, two week ago. *Mucho alto*—w'at you call 'igh op een the air. The hair, she ees black, and hees clothes she ees got on heem moch dus', but ver', ver' good. You know w'at I'm mean?"

"How old was he?"

The man shrugged. "*Quien sabe?* May be t'irty, may be feefty."

"Any baggage?"

"One leetle black—w'at you call heem? Lak these." He indicated an object a foot and a half long. "Weeth 'andle."

"You mean a satchel?"

"Sure; that's heem. Ees buy moch *vino* and eat—ah, *señors*, 'ow she ees eat! Lak the bear w'en she come out een the spreeng."

"Did he give a name?"

"Name? No; but w'atta'ell! That ees nossing. She ees stay t'ree day and night and rest; then she ees ride to the south."

Barry questioned him further, but got no more information. He was satisfied, though, that this was his man, and rewarded the bartender liberally.

Morning found them on their way, eager, alert, anxious to overcome the handicap of a long start. Clues they picked up at almost every stopping point. Frothingham was traveling leisurely now. Presently the trail began to veer to the east, then towards the northeast.

"Doublin' back to the Border," said Barry. "Boys, he's foxy."

They traveled fast, and finally were forced to purchase fresh horses at a *rancho*. From then on they rapidly cut down the distance between them and their quarry. And at last they rode into a town just twelve hours after Frothingham had left it.

"We'll stop here and rest tonight," said Barry. "We're close to him now, and must be fresh for a last dash. Tomorrow we should overtake him."

Late the next evening they entered another town. It was quite a large one, with a number of *cantinas* any one of which might shelter Frothingham. Tuck, who was not so well known by the banker, was sent ahead to investigate the first of these, and returned with the information that Frothingham was not there. They rode to the place, stabled their horses, and had supper in a private room. Over the meal they made their plans.

"Tonight we'll separate and investigate every *cantina* in the town," Barry told them. "This room will be our headquarters. If you spot him, come here and wait for the others. We have no authority to take him, but when he leaves we'll nab him and ride straight to the Border."

One at a time they left the room, each following a course which had been laid out for him.

Barry went into one saloon after the other, carefully surveyed their occupants, and exchanged words with bartenders and others who might have seen the tall American. Nowhere could he find a trace of the cashier; but the hunch that Frothingham was in this town, perhaps within a stone's throw of him, remained. He returned to the room confidant that one of the other three searchers would have located him. One by one they returned, all reporting failure.

"He is in town," said Barry doggedly. "Go out and look again. You may have missed a place."

He started all over, making the round of the *cantinas* he had already visited, questioning an occasional loiterer in the street, but without any success. On a corner he stopped to roll a cigarette, hardly knowing where next to inquire. From within the building behind him came the soft sound of music, the twang of guitars. He dropped the cigarette and turned to stare.

It was the largest place of its kind in the town, being dignified by the title of hotel. Barry had visited its barroom twice; now he decided to try it a third time. He stepped through the low doorway into the hazy atmosphere of the room. The music seemed to come from some place adjacent to the saloon. He bought a drink and casually inquired. The music, he was informed, originated in the dining room where, if he felt inclined to eat, he might secure good food and entertainment. There was a passage from the saloon which he might use. Barry passed through the doorway indicated into a gloomy corridor, came to a pair of soiled velvet hangings, parted them and peered into the dining room.

The place was in semi-darkness, the only illumination besides the stage lights being a single candle on each table. By this light the patrons ate their suppers to the accompaniment of music and dancing. Most of the occupants were in the shadow, but Barry was able to distinguish the features of those nearest him, and when one of these suddenly thrust his face near the candle he gave a gasp of surprise. Never could he forget that huge head with its dark bushy eyebrows and heavy black beard. The man was Tug Groody.

Tug's avid gaze was fixed on the back of a man at a nearby table, a man who dined alone. Barry felt his blood tingle. An instant later this man turned to summon a waiter, and Barry recognized Frothingham.

Instantly he planned his course of action, but even as he was about to retrace his steps to the barroom, Tug got to his feet and crossed the floor to the table at which sat the banker. His face was in the darkness now, but Barry saw his outthrust hand, caught the start which Frothingham gave as he looked up at the man standing by his chair, His own hand came out reluctantly, and Tug sank into a vacant chair, calling to a waiter to move his dinner to the place he now occupied.

Barry retraced his steps to the saloon, went outside, and entered what served as a lobby. He asked for a room and was given a key. Putting it into a pocket, he moved to a chair which stood in a gloomy corner, seated himself, and drew his hat brim over his eyes as though to doze. Through the open doorway which led to the dining room he could see Tug and Frothingham at their table. They were talking earnestly. Presently they got up and came towards the door. Barry slid down in his chair and tried to appear inconspicuous. They came into the lobby, arguing in low voices, and turned to the stairs without looking in his direction.

As soon as they had passed out of sight, Barry got up, yawned, and followed them. The upstairs corridor was empty, but he could hear their voices behind one of the closed doors. Quickly he descended to the ground floor, and, passing out into the street, hurried to the room where they were to meet. Clay was waiting there, but Nip and Tuck had not returned. Barry waited impatiently for five minutes.

"Can't wait any longer; they may leave. When the boys come in, get the horses and come to the hotel. I'll be outside or in the lobby."

As soon as he entered the hotel he realized that something was wrong. A number of employees were gathered at the foot of the stairs, talking excitedly in Spanish, and above their shrill voices he could hear the sound of oaths, the crashing of furniture, and the thud of heavy blows. Passing through them, he dashed up the steps and tried the door from beyond which came the noise. It was locked. Barry backed away, gathered himself for a spring. From within the room came the sullen boom of a heavy shot and the cry of a man mortally wounded.

Barry flung himself at the door, kept battering at it until it was torn from its hinges. He stumbled into the room, caught his balance, glanced swiftly about him.

The place was a wreck. The bed had collapsed and lay in a heap, the washstand had been overturned, the heavy pitcher broken to bits. Across a splintered chair lay Frothingham, clothes almost torn from his body, a crimson splotch on his breast. Barry ran to him, laid him on the floor, slipped an arm under his shoulders and raised him.

There was no water in the room, and not a soul had mounted the stairs to help him. He called, but still no one responded, although he could hear their excited voices. Swearing softly, he was about to lower the man and go for assistance when he saw Frothingham's eyes open. The man gasped, spoke chokingly.

"Tug—Tug—Groody!"

"I know. Talk fast, Frothingham, you haven't much time. This bank failure: it was planned by Horace Moley, wasn't it?"

The man's eyes flamed. "Yes! He—wanted—Basin. Double—crosser. Killed   Slater—killed—me."   He choked again and went limp.

Barry glanced desperately about him. If only he had a witness to Frothingham's confession! He ran to the door and shouted in Spanish for somebody to come. Steps sounded on the stairs and a slick-haired Mexican appeared at the doorway. Barry spoke to him in English, but the man shrugged.

"No hablo Ingles."

Barry swore softly and felt in a pocket. From it he drew a pencil and a scrap of paper. Quickly he wrote:

I, Alonzo J. Frothingham, hereby state with my dying breath that the failure of my bank was planned by Horace Moley in order that he might gain possession of the ranches in Mescal Basin.

Frothingham opened his eyes again as Barry raised him, but they were glazing rapidly and Weston realized with a sinking of spirit that the man could no longer see. Raising Frothingham's right arm, Barry placed the pencil in the lax fingers.

"It's a confession involving Moley," he said quickly. "Can you hear me? Sign it!"

Frothingham nodded weakly, tried to grip the pencil; but it fell from his fingers. Barry recovered it, thrust it back into his grasp.

"For God's sake pull yourself together! As you hope for salvation, sign this!"

Frothingham was rolling his head and moaning, evidently making a great effort to obey. His face contorted, his fingers closed on the pencil, he half raised himself from Barry's supporting arm. Calling quickly in Spanish to the staring Mexican, Barry ordered him to hold Frothingham erect. Placing the paper against the banker's leg, he seized his right hand and attempted to steady it while Frothingham wrote; but the man had exhausted every atom of strength he possessed. Abruptly he collapsed, the hand slipping from Barry's grasp, the whole frame of him going lax. His head lolled to one side and hung there.

The Mexican swore and released his hold. "It is of no use," he said in Spanish. "The man is dead."

Barry got slowly to his feet. Surely the devil was on Moley's side. With that confession he could have put the lawyer behind the bars and saved the Basin to its original owners; but Frothingham had sighed out his last breath in the very act of signing the accusing statement.

People were milling about the door now, and a

pompous little man in the uniform of a policeman was asking questions in rapid-fire Spanish. The man who had ventured upstairs after Barry, and whom Barry gathered was the proprietor of the hotel, answered as rapidly. Weston, meanwhile, hunted for the black satchel. It was not in the room.

His gaze found the open window, and he crossed to it. Within six feet of the opening was the flat roof of an adobe one-story building. To this Tug had leaped and thus reached the street.

Barry pushed through the crowd at the doorway and ran down the stairs. He met Nip and Tuck at the bottom.

"The horses—you have them?"

"Outside. Clay's holdin' them. What happened?"

Barry explained tersely while they raced for the street. As they reached it a horseman rounded the corner of the hotel and went racing along the road to the north. It was dark, but Barry recognized the big figure of Tug Groody.

They flung themselves on their horses and flashed in pursuit. Once clear of the town they spread out, determined to prevent the man doubling on his trail; but after a while Barry called them together again. This murder had been committed in Mexico; Tug's only hope of safety lay in crossing the Border. Occasionally the purusers halted their horses to listen, and always was flung back to them the steady beat of hoofs that told of Tug's flight.

"If we can stick with him until daylight we have him!" shouted Barry.

The stars began to fade. One by one they disappeared as the faintest of gray lights appeared in the east. The light became tinged with rose, and finally the sun ushered in a new day. Once more Barry halted his men. From far ahead of them and to their left came the faint sound of hoofbeats.

"He's off the trail," said Clay, and pointed to the road which, at this point, turned to the right. It was the first short-cut Tug had attempted.

Their horses were nearing exhaustion, but they urged them in pursuit once more. Tug could not keep up that pace much longer. The earth beneath them began to change character; patches of sand appeared, and presently the horses were struggling through great areas of it. The vegetation had dwindled to greasewood and mesquite.

At last they topped a long rise to look down a slope which ended at the edge of a wide, shallow river. And at the foot of the incline rode Tug Groody, his quirt rising and falling, his face turning at intervals to watch the pursuers who had clung to him so tenaciously through the night.

They thundered down the grade, gaining on Tug at every jump. They saw him reach the edge of the river, saw the horse falter and try to swerve. With a strong arm Groody held him to his course, cursing and punishing him with lash and spur. The water flew as the animal struck it; he surged into it with huge leaps—leaps which gradually became weaker. In the middle of the stream he stopped, settled to his withers. Tug was screaming, what it was they did not know.

At the last moment Barry saw the danger and sawed his mount to a squatting stop. "Don't go in!" he called sharply. "Quicksand!"

From the edge of the treacherous shoal they watched, unable to help. Tug was far beyond reach of the strongest rope thrower. The water had covered the horse's back, and Tug had turned in the saddle to untie something he carried behind the cantle. A moment later they saw it was a black satchel. With it in his grasp, the outlaw slipped from his horse. The water must have been shallower than he thought, for they plainly saw the look of consternation which crossed his face as his boots sank in the soft, gripping sand. He floundered about helplessly, his despairing cry reaching them. The horse had been squealing in terror; now, as though resigned to its fate, it was silent, only its head above the placid water. Tug, still gripping the bag, had sunk to his shoulders.

"He's a goner," said Clay tightly. "Barry, ain't there anything we can do for him?"

Barry shook his head, his own face white. There was nothing about them but sand; not a standing bit of timber from which they might break a limb, not a bit of driftwood within range of their vision. Moving to a favorable place, Barry raised his six-gun, took deliberate aim, and fired. The horse gave one convulsive surge, then its head disappeared beneath the surface.

"Shoot me too!" cried Tug. "For Gawd's sake shoot me! Don't let me die like this! Here! Take the damned money. All of it. You can have it all!" He flung the satchel from him. It dropped to the water within six feet of him, floated sluggishly, half submerged. Only Tug's face with its staring, desperate eyes remained above the surface.

Barry, sick at heart, turned his back, and the others did likewise. Clay had closed his eyes and was holding his hands over his ears. Nip and Tuck were pacing back and forth, swearing monotonously.

Tug screamed frantically. "Don't go away! Don't leave me, boys! Shoot me; for Gawd's sake shoot me! Do somethin'! For Gawd's sake do somethin'!"

"Tie your ropes together," snapped Barry. "I'm goin' to where it's solid footin' and try floatin' down to him. If I can get a rope around him maybe we can drag him out."

"Better not try it," advised Nip. "He'll drag you down with him."

"I won't go near him. I'll let the end of the rope drift down to him. Come on; we haven't much time."

They got the ropes and ran upstream as they knotted them together. When at last they found a place where the footing was firm, Barry removed his clothes, waded to the middle, and lay on his back. Slowly he floated down stream, Tug's shrieks ringing in his ears. Abruptly they ceased.

"He's gone," came Clay's voice from the bank. "Tie the rope around you and we'll pull you in."

Barry turned on his side. "I'll make a try for that satchel first."

"It's gone too."

Barry rolled over on his stomach and drifted over the spot where the unfortunate horse and its rider had disappeared. Keeping his eyes open, he scanned the blue bottom. Not a trace of horse, man, or satchel could he perceive; nothing but blue silt waiting to grip him in its implacable clutch. Presently he saw by the nature of the bottom that the footing was safe, so he stood erect and waded ashore.

"We'll try for the satchel farther down stream," he told them. "It might have drifted clear of the quicksand."

"You goin' to try to recover Moley's money for him?"

"Not for him," said Barry bitterly. "After what he has done he sure isn't entitled to recover it. If we find it we will use it to redeem those notes he holds."

They started at a point two miles below the quicksand bar, stripping and wading back and forth across the shallow river, gradually working up-stream. It was slow work, and they consumed the whole day at it. Defeated, they finally abandoned the search and rode back to the nearest town to replenish their supplies. Dejectedly they started for home. Nearly four weeks had passed since they had left the Basin.

For fully half a day they rode almost in silence; then Nip swore fervently and delivered himself.

"What's the use of bein' downhearted? Dang it, there's a sun in the sky somewhere, and I ain't never met up with a rascal yet that didn't git his just deserts in the long run. Come on, Tuck; let's sing.

"Oh, I onct loved Caroline Durkus,
Bought a ring and a nice little home;
But she married a freak from the circus,
So I rambled to old Wyom'."

Four days later they rode wearily up the trail to the Cinchbuckle ranch house to find Barbara awaiting them. Her face was pale, but she held her head high. They dismounted slowly, and Barry told her of their experiences.

"Always too late," he finished bitterly. "Too late to hear Slater's story, too late to get Frothingham's confession, too late to recover the money from Tug. And our hands are tied. Frothingham confessed to me; we know Moley is behind the whole thing, but we can't even begin to prove it. Barbara, I reckon I've failed you; nothin' but a miracle can save the Cinchbuckle now."

She came over to him and placed a hand gently on his shoulder.

"Don't think of the Cinchbuckle, Barry. Oh, I wish that were all we had to worry about! But it isn't. Barry, it hurts me to tell you, but you must know. While you were gone your mother deeded the Flying W to Horace Moley."

He started as though stung. "My mother—deeded the Flyin' W?"

"Yes. Lola told me about it. Moley presented a note your step-father had executed before he disappeared. It wasn't binding on your mother, but she declared it would be honored, that she had taken her oath before God to share with her husband poverty or wealth."

"How much was the note for?" asked Barry dully.

"Ten thousand dollars."

He turned away and stared for a moment over the rolling rangeland.

"Thanks, Barbara," he said, and abruptly left them.

CHAPTER XVII

THE BLUFF THAT WORKED

IT was a thoroughly dejected Barry Weston who rode to the Flying W that evening. This was the crowning blow. Had the Flying W remained, he had intended to ask Barbara to share it with them; now it seemed that he and his mother would be as homeless as she.

Lola saw him ride into the yard and came running to meet him. There was a smile of welcome on her lips, but the lovely eyes were clouded.

"Oh, Bar-ree!" she cried, and flung herself into his arms. He held her absently, patting her shoulder.

"How is ma?"

"She ees not well, but brave. Ah, Bar-ree, she ees won'erful! Ees break her 'eart to let go the *rancho,* for she ees theenk of you all the tam; but she say she can not do anything else. These step-father of yours, he ees a peeg! I'm lak to scratch hees eyes out."

"Lola, I reckon I could watch you do it and feel right happy about it. But the thing's done, and we mustn't let her see how badly we feel."

"You 'ad no luck weeth the man you 'unt?"

"No." He told her about it while he off-saddled and cared for his tired horse. They walked to the house together.

"Me, I'm feex you nice dinner. You go to your *madre;* she weel be glad to see you. Bar-ree, these 'Orace Moley ees mak her all upset."

He nodded and went into her room. She had heard his voice and was waiting for him. Kneeling, he let her take him in her arms and cry over him for a little while, then disengaged himself and looked at her severely.

"Doctor Barry Q. Weston back on the job again," he told her. "No more tears, young lady! How's the appetite? and have you been takin' your exercise?"

She smiled through her tears. "Lola has been very kind to me, Barry; but, oh, Barry! we've lost our home. I had to give up the one thing I had been saving so carefully for you."

"Shucks, that's nothin' to worry about. What's a few hundred acres of dry land and a hatful of skinny cows? Forget it, lady. You've spent most of your life in the Basin as it is; it's time you had a change. I'm goin' to take you up into Montana—let you see some new country. Now dry those eyes. Shame on you, carryin' on like this, and you a pioneer! Get that chin up."

Although the heart within him was sick, he stayed with her joking and laughing until the sparkle came back to her eyes, the faint color to her cheeks. Lola brought a tray with her supper, and added her smile and word of cheer. Deftly and tenderly she arranged the covers, then seated herself by the bed.

"Your supper ees on the table," she told Barry. "Go eat eet; I weel stay weeth your *madre*. We are ver' good frien's, *madre* and me; no?"

Barry's mother laid a white hand on Lola's brown one. "She has been very sweet, Barry; she has cared for me as though she were my own daughter."

"See?" cried Lola. "Barbara, she ees my sister, and 'ere I'm fin' a *madre*. All I'm need now ees w'at you call father and I'm got 'ole fam'ly."

"Where do I come in?" asked Barry.

For an instant she sobered, regarding him from her big eyes with a look that he could not fathom; then she laughed again and answered gaily.

"You are my bro-ther; my nice, beeg bro-ther. I'm ver' proud of heem."

Their banter, together with the excellent supper Lola had prepared, helped to dispel to a great extent his dejection. As he ate, he thought. Moley had triumphed; the Basin spreads were his even to the Flying W. Deceit, treachery, fraud—all had been combined to bring about his victory; yet, with all this double-dealing, Moley must have left a loophole. Man is by no means a perfect creature; somewhere there must have been a slip. But where?

Steve, of course, would know things; but Steve was in the game and he would not talk. Tug Groody and Frothingham were gone. So was Sam Hodge. There remained his step-father and possibly Ace Polmateer. The former had disappeared, although Barry did not believe he had gone far. Chet Lewis was too timid and entirely unused to depending upon himself.

Ace and his gunmen? The former might know something, but Barry did not credit the two bouncers with Horace Moley's confidence. One thing they did know, and that was the truth about Garth's killing. This angle was brought more strongly to his mind when Nip and Tuck arrived at the ranch.

"Barry," said Nip, "Clement's trial comes up tomorrow. Barbara didn't say anything to you, but she's worried sick. Seems like Horace Moley made her some kind of a proposition whereby he'd git Clement off if she deeded the ranch over to him. Said somethin' about witnesses bein' mistaken. She turned him down cold."

"Now that Sam Hodge is dead, Ace and his bouncers are the ones who will convict him." For a short space Barry stood looking at the darkening horizon; then he made a sudden gesture and spoke shortly. "Get Lola to fix you some supper, then saddle up fresh horses. We're goin' to Mescal."

As they were about to enter the house, Lola came to the door. Tuck nodded and tipped his hat; Nip walked swiftly to her and stood looking down into her pert face.

"Lola! Ain't you glad to see me?"

She permitted a look of puzzlement to cross her face. "Who he ees? He spik to me lak he know me. Ah! I 'ave eet! Ees the beeg *vaquero* who work for Bar-ree Wes-ton. Lemme see; ees eet Neep or Tuck?"

"Aw, Lola, quit your funnin'. You know who I am. Gosh; I'd hoped you would miss me like I missed you."

He appeared so crest-fallen that Lola relented. Her eyes softened and she placed a hand on his arm.

"Of a certainty I know. You are Neep, my ver' good frien'. And I'm mees you 'ole, 'ole lot. Now you come een, and we feex the supper, no?"

An hour later Barry and the two cowboys were riding slowly towards Mescal. As they rode he outlined his plan. It was a desperate one, but they adopted it without protest.

"Ace and his gunmen, Cliff Bender and Doug Pell, are the ones who know about that holstered gun. As sure as they testify Clem will be convicted. I aim to prevent their testifyin'. Nobody in town knows we have returned, and I told Lola to ride to the Cinchbuckle and warn Clay to keep out of sight. What we must manage to do is to get the three of them and take them to that line cabin on the Cinchbuckle south range and keep them there. If we're lucky we can force an adjournment or a postponement of the trial."

Tuck swore. "And if we apply a couple of hot irons in the right place, mebbe we can force the truth from one of them."

"I've half a mind to try. The whole deal has been a crooked one from the start, and one way of fightin' fire is with fire."

They talked it over, holding their horses to a walk. When they finally picked up the lights of the town they halted and dismounted. They were in no hurry to reach Mescal. It was close to one in the morning when they resumed their way. Circling the town, they approached it from the west, halting again in the dark-

ness behind the hotel stable. Barry advanced on foot
and investigated, finding the stable deserted save for
the horses which were kept there. Among these were
two belonging to Bender and Pell. Working silently,
he found saddles and bridles, and, after adjusting
them, led the two animals to where their own mounts
were waiting. Returning to the barn, he selected a horse
and outfit for Ace Polmateer.

"We better get to work," he told his companions as
he rejoined them. "The lights are out except for a
couple in the rear. Tie those horses good."

As silently as three shadows they stole past the
barn and along the side of the hotel. At the front
corner was the room of the two gunmen. Is was the
only bedroom on the first floor, and was used by them
in order that they might be near the safe where Ace
locked the day's receipts.

The routine followed by Polmateer each night was
well enough known to them. At closing time the bouncers shook the sleepers into life and sent them staggering
on their way. The doors were locked and they remained
with Ace while he checked with his gamblers and
counted the contents of the till. The three then walked
to the hotel where Ace put the money in the safe and
ascended the stairs to his room on the second floor.

At a window of the gunmen's room they halted.

"Open," said Barry, and lifted himself to the sill.
Nip and Tuck followed, and, according to their plan,
remained in the dark room. Barry peered through the
front doorway. The clerk had gone to bed, leaving a
lamp burning on the counter. Swiftly and noiselessly

Barry slipped into the lobby and ascended the stairs. Ace's door was locked, so he lowered the wick of the corridor lamp until it gave only the feeblest of glows, then stationed himself at the end of the hall nearest the stairs.

Presently he heard low voices and the thud of booted feet. He judged that Ace and the two gunmen had entered the lobby. The click of the safe lock came clearly to him as Ace snapped the handle in place. He heard a careless, *"Hasta Mañana,* boys," grunted replies from the bouncers, and the sound of footsteps on the stairs.

Barry crouched in the shadows and drew his gun. There must be no noise. The footsteps drew nearer, and he heard Ace swear and mutter something about the dimmed light. The next instant he stepped around the corner and brought up against the muzzle of Barry's Colt.

"Not a word," came the whispered command. "Up with your hands."

Ace stood staring, taken entirely by surprise. Slowly his hands crept upward. "You're all wrong, buddy," he whispered. "I haven't a dime on me."

"Turn around."

Ace obeyed, and Barry swiftly tied his hands behind him with a rope he had brought for the purpose. Standing close to the man, his gun pressed against his back, he said, "This is Barry Weston. Know me, don't you? One little peep and I'll drill you. Stand where you are."

Not a sound had reached him from below. Ace stood

stock still; he had been a sure-thing gambler too long to risk taking a chance now. They were at the head of the stairs, and Barry was peering intently at the thin light which illuminated the lobby. Suddenly this was extinguished, and he knew Nip and Tuck had carried out their part of the program. He heard their soft footsteps as they forced the gunmen to walk ahead of them into the dining room and through the kitchen doorway.

"Get goin'," commanded Barry. "Take it easy, and don't make the mistake of thinkin' you can get away."

Taking a couple turns of the rope about his wrist, he followed Ace down the stairs. At the bottom he moved close to him, putting the gunmuzzle against his back. Down the dining room aisle they walked, through the kitchen and into the starlight behind the hotel. Straight to the horses he marched Ace, to find Nip and Tuck with their prisoners awaiting them.

Here the three were searched and their weapons removed. Then, one at a time, they were forced to mount and were tied securely to their horses. A rope around the body of each connected them with their captors. Still enforcing strict silence, they rode slowly across the range, out to the south and east, and finally headed for the Cinchbuckle. Presently the horses were urged to a running walk, and by the time dawn overtook them the cabin was in sight. A man was standing in the doorway awaiting them. It was Clay.

"Got your message," he told Barry. "Thought you might need me."

"Good. Start a fire in the stove and fix some breakfast for us. Don't bother with Ace and his friends; they ain't hungry yet."

The prisoners were allowed to dismount and seat themselves on the ground. Their hands were still tied, and they were not permitted to communicate with each other. Bender and Pell were grinning; Ace's face held a defiant sneer.

"You're wasting time," he told Barry scornfully. "Keeping us from testifying won't help Clement a bit. We gave our testimony at the inquest, and in our absence they'll simply read what we said then into the record."

The blow told, but Barry's face did not betray that fact. "We're not worryin' about that," he said calmly. Nevertheless, when Clay was guarding the prisoners and they were eating their breakfast, he admitted that this contingency had not occurred to him.

"Then we got to git the truth outa them," said Tuck savagely. "Heat up a poker and burn a few fancy crosses on the bottoms of their feet."

"We're supposed to be civilized."

"So are they, but they ain't. And it won't do much damage; we brand cows and they live to eat grass."

"We might bluff them."

"They're too wise to bluff."

"Maybe. Boys, somebody in that outfit reloaded Cal Garth's gun and put it back into his holster; which of the three do you think did it?"

"Ace," answered Nip. "He's the brains of the outfit, and the boss."

"Keno," agreed Tuck. "That's my guess too."

"All right; we'll work it on that theory. This is what we'll do." He went on to explain in a voice too low for any outside to hear.

Presently they got up and walked out to where Ace and his gunmen were seated. They did not seem in the least disturbed. As though in accordance with a pre-arranged plan, Nip and Tuck led the horses off into the brush, returning presently on foot.

Barry addressed them shortly. "All right, boys; take Pell and Bender away. Don't let them talk to each other. I'll be down presently when I'm finished with Ace."

For the first time the sneer left Polmateer's lips. "What are you going to do with me?"

Barry adopted the harshest tone he could command. "Clement Dawn is a friend of ours. We don't aim to stand on one side and see him railroaded on lyin' evidence. Clay is heatin' a poker in the stove, and we aim to get the truth out of you three before we finish. Take 'em away, boys. Ace, walk into the cabin."

For a moment the man stared wildly. "You can't do that! You're bluffing!" Barry had judged him correctly; he was soft and sensitive and had a yellow streak a yard wide.

"Get inside," said Barry, and slapped him across the face. It was an act of which he was not proud, but he was acting a part designed to impress Bender and Pell.

The two protested as their captors relentlessly drove them through the brush to the stagnant pool which lay hardly within shouting distance of the cabin. Here at its edge they were tied to trees some distance apart, while Nip and Tuck grimly seated themselves on the ground. Bender and Pell were no longer grinning.

"You know," said Nip to Tuck, "they oughta repeal that part of the law which forbids torture. A good hot iron can draw more from a man in a minute than a whole flock of prosecutin' attorneys can in a year."

"Trouble is it draws out as many lies as it does truths."

"Yeah, but in time a fella can git to the bottom of things. Take this case. Barry ain't aimin' to stop with Ace; he'll take those jiggers and hear what they have to say too. Then he can add up the stories and strike an average." Glancing carelessly at the two gunmen, Nip caught the swift apprehensive looks they exchanged.

And then there came to them the sound of a cry of sheer agony. The shriek was muffled by distance, but there was no mistaking the note of horrible pain and fear it held. The two gunmen started, and Bender struggled fiercely with his bonds.

"Hold still," said Nip, "or I'll bust you over the head with a rock. You think Ace is bein' tortured; well, what about Miss Dawn and all of Clement's friends? You dirty low-down skunks were fixin' to torture them a million times worse by sendin' Clement to the gallows with your lyin' testimony. For gosh sake, take your medicine like men."

Again the agonized cry reached them. Even Nip and Tuck felt the chill creep up their spines. They exchanged uneasy glances; surely such a horrible sound could not be drawn from human lips except through torture. Bender and Pell were standing stiffly, eyes staring, beads of sweat on their brows.

Nip forced himself to speak callously. "Reckon that last touch brought somethin' out, eh, Tuck?"

"Sure. He'll talk. He'll say plenty." Tucked rolled a cigarette and puffed on it thoughtfully. "Stinks like heck down here," he complained.

"That's the comp'ny you're smellin'.'"

Presently they heard the sounds of a man approaching through the brush, and Barry stepped into sight. His face was drawn in harsh lines and his eyes burned. He stood looking from one to the other of the gunmen.

"Ace talk?" inquired Nip.

The answer was short. "Yes. Reckon I'll take Bender next."

Bender strained again at his bonds, twisting and writhing, his face livid. "You ain't gonna torture me!" he screamed. "You can kill me first."

"We could do that long ago if we wanted to," said Barry calmly. "Quiet down or I'll clap you with a gun barrel; then we can tie you to the bunk without any trouble."

"I tell you you won't torture me!" panted Bender. "I'll talk. What is it you want to know?"

"You'll talk all right. Just like Ace. Untie him, boys."

Nip and Tuck started working on the bonds.

"Dang you," growled the former. "You've pulled those knots so tight we'll have to cut 'em. Give him an extry brand for me, Barry."

"Wait a minute!" Bender had suddenly become calm. "I'll bet Ace put the blame on us; didn't he, Weston?"

"I'm not sayin'," answered Barry, but there was a look in his eyes which convinced Bender he had spoken the truth.

"You hear that, Doug? The lousy son blamed us! Well, we didn't do it. We was busy holdin' back the crowd. Ace done it himself. I seen him."

"Hush your mouth!" cried Pell.

"I won't! I ain't gittin' the bottoms of my feet burned for nobody. Tell the truth, Doug. By Godfrey, I will! And I'll tell it under oath."

"Reckon your oath ain't worth much," said Barry. "We'll get the truth in our own way. Cut the rope, Nip."

The man fell to cursing Pell for his failure to support him until finally Doug gave in.

"All right, Weston; you win. Ace reloaded that gun and put it back."

"Untie them both; we'll give them a chance to say that in Ace's presence."

They were forced to lead the way to the cabin. Clay was waiting at the door. "Two of 'em? Well, the more the merrier. Poker's good and hot; bring 'em right in."

They entered the cabin, and even Nip and Tuck for the moment stood appalled. Ace Polmateer was bound to a bunk. His boots and socks had been removed and both feet were roughly bandaged. He lay limp and panting, eyes closed, sweat standing out on his white forehead.

Barry addressed him roughly. "Ace, here are pour two bouncers. We aimed to give them a dose of your medicine, but they swear that you reloaded Garth's gun and put it into his holster."

"It's a lie," said Ace thickly.

"It ain't no lie!" blazed Bender. "You know you did it. I seen you. Me and Doug both."

"Conflictin' stories," said Barry shortly. "Clay, get Ace off there; we'll work on Bender a bit."

"No use," said Pell, his eyes on Ace's bandaged feet. "Ace, you got to take it this time. I figgered they were bluffin', but I see they ain't. I don't aim to be crippled. Take us to town, Weston; we'll testify."

"All right; but we'll put the confession in writin' first."

He found paper and pencil and dictated a short statement for each to sign. The statements were witnessed and pocketed by Barry.

"Stay with Ace, Clay. We'll take 'em in."

The horses were brought up and the five mounted and rode away, the two bouncers again securely tied.

"Better stick to your stories, boys," Barry warned. "If you don't, we'll have the sheriff hold you on the strength of these confessions, and Ace will have a chance to save his hide by blamin' you."

It was their one chance and they took it. A wave of excitement swept the court room when two of the missing witnesses appeared in the custody of their three guards. Barry saw Barbara staring at him, lips parted, a question in her eyes, and smiled reassuringly.

Both the prosecuting attorney and Clement's lawyer rushed to meet them.

The two gunmen went on the stand and in unfaltering voices told of the frame-up, putting the blame on Ace Polmateer. The building rocked with applause and the case was dismissed. Matt Billings promptly placed Bender and Pell under arrest for perjury at the inquest.

Barry and his friends escorted Clement and Barbara from the court room. On the way out they passed Horace Moley and his son. Steve's face was livid, and only his father's restraining hand kept him from leaping at Barry. The lawyer's face was inscrutable, but his burning gaze met Barry's triumphant one and in it Barry read suppressed fury and implacable hate.

They reached the jail just as Matt Billings came out after locking up his prisoners. Barry called to him to join them.

"Got another perjury prisoner for you. Ride with us to the Cinchbuckle south line cabin and I'll turn Polmateer over to you."

Nip and Tuck drew Barry aside. "How are you goin' to explain his burned feet?" they demanded.

Barry chuckled. "Ace isn't hurt a bit; he just thinks he is. You see, I'd heard that if you make a fella believe you're goin' to burn him and then touch him with a piece of ice, he'll think sure enough you used a hot iron. I didn't have any ice, but I put a pewter knife in a bucket of that cold spring water and it served the same purpose. We tied him to the bunk and Clay held the hot poker close to his feet. Then I yelled

'Now!' and touched him with the cold knife handle. He sure hollered."

Nip shuddered at the memory. "I'll say he hollered! You must have touched his conscience. I always figgered he carried it in his feet."

CHAPTER XVIII

THE SECRET OF THE POOL

T HE days which immediately followed the trial of Clement Dawn were heart-breaking ones for the Basin ranchers. Horace Moley sued for judgment against the Cinchbuckle and secured it. The other spreads had been deeded to him; now the Cinchbuckle was sold by the sheriff and bid in by Steve Moley. Together Steve and his father owned the entire Basin. The ranchers had been given a month in which to settle up their affairs, pack their personal belongings, and get out.

Barry and his two cowboys were making a final tour of the property in a last effort to determine just what the valuable thing was they were sure the Basin held. The matter intrigued Barry; he was convinced that Moley would never have gone to the lengths he had for the simple purpose of acquiring cattle range.

"You say there were no signs of gold or silver?" questioned Nip.

"Not a sign; and I don't know what else it could be." Barry rode for a short space in silence, mentally going over every inch of ground he had covered, searching for the tiniest clue to Slater's secret. The man had found something, and had been paid five thousand dollars for his find; Barry was positive of that. The memory came to him of a dank, stagnant pool which stank, and suddenly he jerked erect in the saddle.

"Come with me," he said tersely, and headed for the line cabin.

Not a word could they get out of him until they stood by the side of the evil-smelling pool. Barry scanned the surface of the water and exclaimed aloud.

"That's it! That's the secret! And I sat here a half hour and didn't see it."

"See what?" asked Nip.

Barry pointed. "That film over there. No wonder the motto was 'Buy, steal, or kill'! How blind I've been! And now Moley—"

"What in heck are you talkin' about? What film?"

"You're dumb as I am, Nip. That rainbow film on the top of the water over in that dark corner. It's there plain as day and cryin' to be noticed. You can even smell it."

"Smell it?" Nip sniffed the air, then stiffened like a pointer. "Holy bobcats! Tuck, you danged fool, it's *oil!*"

"Oil!"

Barry spoke bitterly. "Oil. The whole Basin's undermined with it, likely. And if we had only used our eyes and our noses we could have got plenty of capital to take care of those notes. Now Moley and his son are headed towards millions while the ones to whom it really belongs are without even homes to live in!"

He turned to them suddenly. "Boys, keep this to yourselves. Moley got possession by fraud; somewhere he must have tripped up. We missed out on Frothingham and Hodge and Groody; but there must be somebody alive that we can squeeze evidence from."

"Who could it be besides Steve?"

"My step-father for one. It's a slim chance; Horace Moley would hardly trust him, but he was paid ten thousand dollars for somethin'. Boys, I'm goin' after him right now."

He rode off without another word, and for a long time the two cowboys sat at the edge of the pool and studied the film on its surface.

"Tuck," sighed Nip, "we're the two biggest fools unhung. We set tight while Barry was puttin' ice packs on Ace's feet and looked right at a hundred million dollars without seein' it. Moley sure rooked us good. And he killed Slater so's he wouldn't have to share it."

"Be a damn' good joke on him if Slater had rooked him," said Tuck savagely.

"How'd he do it? He couldn't keep pourin' oil on top of the water right along, and there's enough overflow to the creek to run it off."

There was a period of silence; then—"I know one way he could do it," said Nip, and proceeded to explain.

Barry, in the meanwhile, had started his search. He did not believe his step-father would go very far, and dismissed at once the possibility of his fleeing to Mexico. He met people in Mescal who had seen Chet Lewis ride north. At Hartsville he learned that Lewis had purchased some supplies. From Hartsville he traced him to Juniper, and there lost him; but north of Juniper was the large town of Benson, and here Barry began a systematic search which finally led him to his man.

Chet was seated in an obscure table in the corner of a saloon. He was slumped in his chair and his head was lowered. For Chet was lonesome; even with a thousand dollars he was lonesome. He had lost his home and what friends he had, and he must stretch that thousand a long way. Here he didn't know a soul and was afraid to scrape up an acquaintance lest the money be taken from him. He heard the rasp of a chair on the far side of his table and looked up. Barry Weston was standing there watching him.

With a cry of alarm Chet started to his feet, but Barry reached out and gripped him by the wrist. "Sit down, Chet; I'm not goin' to hurt you. I just want to ask you some questions."

Chet sank back into the chair, and Barry seated himself opposite him.

"Chet, you gave Horace Moley a note, didn't you?"

"Why—why, yes; I reckon I did."

"Do you know what use he made of it? He presented it to my mother for payment, and she, not having the money, deeded the Flying W over to him. That is how she stood by you, Chet, after the dirty way you treated her."

Chet was sputtering. "But—but, Barry, she hadn't oughta done that! The note wasn't for much."

Barry smiled mirthlessly. "No, not much; just a mere ten thousand dollars."

"*Ten* thousand dollars! Barry, that ain't so! That note was for *one* thousand dollars. I swear it was!"

Barry's eyes kindled. "One thousand! Chet, are you sure?"

"Of course I'm sure. I signed it, didn't I? And I sure can read. Moley paid me one thousand dollars; I got most of it yet."

"Why did he pay you that amount? Tell the truth now!"

Chet did. "I thought they were goin' to take you away and warn you not to come back," he whined. "Honest I did, Barry."

"Forget it." Again Barry had failed to uncover any evidence of fraud on Moley's part, so far as acquiring the Basin land was concerned; but he had something to hold over the lawyer if Lewis were speaking the truth: forgery.

"Chet, if you're lyin' to me I'll forget you're my mother's husband!"

"I ain't lyin'. He gave me one thousand dollars, and I signed a note for that amount. I'll face him if you say so."

Barry got up. "Get your horse and we'll ride."

They reached Mescal early in the morning and continued on to the Flying W. Barry's mother produced the canceled note, and Chet scanned it briefly.

"That looks like my signature, but it ain't. I never signed this note."

"Then it's forgery." Barry's eyes were glinting. "I believe we have the wolf by the nape of the neck at last. Lola, where are Nip and Tuck?"

"They are gone long tam, Bar-ree. The day you lef' they come 'ere and get the shovel and the peek. Nex' day they come back, mak me feex them moch food, an' go away weeth the wagon. I'm not see them seence."

"If they show up send them to Mescal. Come on, Chet."

Back to town they rode and stopped at the sheriff's office. Here they repeated the story of the forged note. Matt's face lighted up.

"Barry, you got him hooked. He'll be a long time explainin' this away. I'll go with you."

Horace Moley opened the door to his office. The faintest perceptible start was the only sign to betray any apprehension he might have felt at sight of Chet Lewis.

"I'm quite busy today," he said. "Can't you return later?"

"This business won't wait," Barry told him, and pushed by him into the room. The others followed, and Moley reluctantly seated himself at his desk.

"It's about this note for ten thousand dollars," said Barry, and spread the paper on the desk before Moley. "Chet Lewis declares the signature has been forged."

"Chet Lewis lies," said Moley calmly. "I paid him ten thousand dollars for improvements on the Fly-in' W."

"Chet didn't own the Flyin' W."

"His wife did. I took a chance on her honoring the note. You must admit my judgment was good." Moley had entirely recovered his confidence.

"Your judgment was excellent, Moley. The whole plan was a good one. Tom Slater found oil in the Basin—"

"Oil!" exclaimed both Matt and Lewis.

"Yes, oil. You, Moley, paid him five thousand for the secret and then had Tug Groody rub him out so he wouldn't talk. You started a bank with Frothingham the apparent owner. He lent money recklessly on demand notes. When the money was spent, he disappeared and you turn up the real owner. You pose as a man greatly wronged, and call the notes to save you from ruin. They are not honored, and the collateral is forfeited. You now own the whole Basin, you and your son, and the oil which lies under it. Well worked out, Moley; and absolutely foolproof."

Moley answered tightly. "You'll pay for those wild statements, Weston! I'll sue you for everything you own or hope to own."

Barry laughed bitterly. "Go ahead and sue; you've already taken everything. All that is left to me is the satisfaction of branding you the dirty crook you are. Wallow in your oil if you want to; but make up your mind to spend some of your life behind the bars for forgery. Where's that other note? The one Chet really signed?"

"This is the only note. Now get out of my office, all of you. Here! What are you doing?" For Barry, ignoring the command, had stepped past the desk and was drawing open the heavy iron door to the safe.

Moley sprang up, but Matt Billings gave him a shove which sent him back into his chair. "Set quiet, Horace. It's your turn to squirm."

"You too, eh? A fine sheriff you are! Here is a man thrusting himself unbidden into my office and going through my private papers. I'll have you removed from office for this."

Matt only glared at him, and Horace was forced to sit idly and fume while Barry systematically went through his papers.

"Here it is," Weston said at last. "A note for one thousand dollars."

Chet Lewis examined it and nodded. "That's the one I signed."

"I reckon, Horace," said Barry quietly, "that you'd better deed the Flyin' W back to my mother."

Moley sprang to his feet, his face blazing. "I'll do nothing of the sort! This is a frame-up, and I'll fight it to the last court. The Flying W is mine, legally mine, and so is the rest of the Basin. Yes, there is oil there, and I intend to have it. Every barrel—every pint! And when I get it, I'll hound you and every miserable cur in your pack until I put them where they belong!"

The office door opened, and two men entered.

"Did I hear somethin' about oil?" asked Nip.

Barry looked at them. Their eyes were very bright and they seemed to be laboring under some excitement.

Nip spoke to Tuck. "Did you hear what I heard?

He's gonna git every barrel—every pint! Oh, my gosh! What a joke."

Moley spoke sharply. "Joke? What do you mean?"

Nip answered pityingly. "Horace, in some ways you're a smart man; but in others you're a plain danged fool. Do you think a fella like Slater would part with a secret like that for five thousand dollars? He sure rooked you good! And you countin' on all that oil, all them untold millions locked in the bosom of Mother Earth! Oh, my gosh!"

Moley leaped forward and seized him. "What are you saying?" he demanded harshly. "Talk, damn you! What are you hinting at?"

Nip brushed him aside. "Hands off, sucker, you'll git me dirty. I ain't *hintin'* at nothin'; I'm talkin' right out in meetin'. There's more oil in that lamp over there than in the whole danged Basin. Slater just rooked you for five thousand bucks."

Moley gasped, staggered back against the desk. "You're lying! The seepage—I saw it with my own eyes; not once, but many times. He couldn't have put it there and kept it there for a year."

"Hold your damned tongue!" came a harsh command from the doorway. Steve Moley had entered the room. "What's this you're talkin' about, Nip?"

Horace was pale and shaken. "They say there is no oil, Stevie. I can't believe it."

"They're lyin'. They're makin' a fool of you. Can't you see it's a put-up job to make you admit—" He broke off suddenly.

"Admit what?" snapped Barry.

"Nothin'."

"Steve," said Nip, "if it wasn't such a good joke on you I'd call your hand. Better look for yourself before you call any more names."

"Look where?"

"Where do you think? In that little pond near the Cinchbuckle south line cabin. Come on; let's all take a look."

Horace Moley's face was pinched and drawn. "See? They know about the pool, Stevie. I must see; I must see for myself!"

They passed out of the office together, Barry and Matt bright-eyed, Nip and Tuck chuckling over their joke, the lawyer and his son harsh-faced and anxious. Moley's buggy was prepared and a pick and shovel tossed into the box. Horace driving the rig and the other six riding, they started on their trip.

It was noon when they reached the cabin. Here they got down and pushed their way through the brush to the edge of the stagnant pool. It's green-scummed surface was placid; the tell-tale film of oil still spread itself across the little corner Slater had first pointed out.

The two cowboys led the way to a point some ten feet above the surface of the water and silently indicated the freshly turned earth.

"We opened her up once," said Nip, "but it was such a good joke that we covered it again. Start diggin', Horace."

It was Horace who seized the pick and started to work. Steve shoveled. They did not have far to dig.

Presently the pick struck wood, and a little later the head of a barrel was uncovered.

"Keep diggin'," said Tuck grinning. "Might as well git the whole of the bad news in a lump."

Shoveling feverishly, Steve uncovered the front of the barrel; then stood staring down at his feet. He swore harshly and climbed from the hole. Without a word he strode away, crashing through the brush, and a moment later they heard the thud of his horse's hoofs.

Horace Moley looked into the hole, and as he gazed he seemed to grow infinitely older. The lines in his lean face became deeper, the mouth drew down at the corners, the whole lank frame seemed to shrink.

"See how it's worked?" asked Nip cheerfully. "Right here is a nice big barrel of crude oil, buried above the water line. From the bunghole in the bottom runs a rubber hose. If you dig it up you'll see that it ends below the surface of the pond. The oil from the barrel runs through the hose and slowly seeps through the ground into the pool. There, bein' lighter than water, it rises to the top and spreads itself in that purty film which led our friend Horace to commit all kinds of meanness. Nice, ain't it?"

The life seemed to return to Horace Moley. Eyes blazing, jaws tight, he cursed the man he blamed for the tragedy. "The damned double-crosser! The cursed rattlesnake! The poisonous skunk! He fooled me—tricked me—bled me! Blast his lying heart!"

Matt Billings was grinning. "Go on, Horace; git it outa your system. It's so illuminatin' to hear a pious soul like you talk about foolin' and trickin' and bleedin'. And when you run plumb outa steam, you can drive back to Mescal and see if the judge will turn you loose on bail. I reckon you can gather from that that I'm arrestin' you for forgery."

CHAPTER XIX

RETRIBUTION

WHEN Horace Moley left the court house after posting bond, folks noticed the change which had come over him. He no longer walked erect, stepping briskly along the street; his shoulders sagged, his lean face was haggard, and he shuffled his feet as though too weary to raise them.

"Jest like a wolf slinkin'," someone remarked.

At the Palace he turned mechanically towards the doorway for his customary Scotch and soda. As the doors parted, he halted. Steve was seated at a table, a bottle before him, hand clutched tightly about a glass, eyes fixed on the blank wall of the saloon.

Horace backed away, his eyes pain-stricken. For a moment he stood outside the Palace, hesitant, a bit bewildered. So crushing had been his disappointment, so staggering the wreck of his dreams, that he was no longer complete master of himself. Somewhere a thread had snapped. At last he stepped into the road and shuffled through the dust to his office. The wolf, mortally wounded, had slunk to his lair.

Inside the room, he seated himself at his desk and began mechanically to sort the contents of the drawers. He uncovered a double-barrelled Derringer and for a moment examined it curiously. For years it had lain there loaded and untouched. He placed it on the top of the desk and covered it with a paper.

A step sounded in the outer room and somebody tried the door. The thought that this was Barry Weston come to taunt him struck the lawyer, and his eyes flamed with their old fire. He placed his hand on the revolver, removed it, saw that the weapon was entirely covered, then arose and went to the door.

It was Steve who entered, and Steve was very drunk. For a moment he stood leering at his father, swaying a bit on his feet, his bloodshot eyes wild.

"Stevie!" faltered Horace, and backed away from him.

Steve swept off his hat and made a bow which nearly proved his undoing.

"Hail to king!" he sneered. "Oil king; mighty Mogul of universe! Hell of a mess you've made of things, ain't you?"

Horace had backed against the desk. "Stevie!" he cried again. "It wasn't my fault. I meant for the best. I wanted you to be rich, to have things, to—to—"

Steve laughed raspingly. "Yeah, you did! You were out to feather your own nest, you danged ol' lobo you! Used ever'body you could get your han's on, me included. Oil! Oil! You danged fool, you oughta knowed Slater 'd never sell a whole Basin of oil for five thousand bucks."

"But that wasn't all he was to have," protested Moley desperately. "I promised him a share—fifty-fifty! You remember, Stevie?"

"Sure; I remem'er. Promised him half, and then had him killed so's you wouldn't have to keep your promise. Great li'l promiser, you are. Been usin' me like the res' of 'em. Puppets; tha's what you called 'em. Jump when you pull string. Took care to be covered up, didn't you? With your phoney bank and your rustlin' and your killin'. All covered up; nobody can prove a thing. But where do puppets come in, huh? Sam and Tug and Frothin'ham dead. Ace in jail. Bascomb lyin' head off to save hisself. And how about me? Know what you've let me in for? I'll tell you. They'll work on Ace and make him tell about that Clement Dawn frame-up. I'll be blamed. Right now they got Hop Finch and Pug Parsons down at sheriff's office puttin' screws to 'em. They'll squeal about Clay Dawn. I'm blamed again. Wes'on seen me rustlin' them Cinchbuckle breeders. Me! Me! I'm one to get it in the neck, not you. Dang your measly soul, I oughta choke life outa you!"

He lurched forward again, and Horace, desperately afraid, unable to retreat farther, grappled with him. His frantic grip infuriated the drunken man. Like one become suddenly insane, Steve twisted and tore and struck, not heeding the feeble cries of his father. Cursing in drunken frenzy, he pressed the frail lawyer back on the desk. Horace Moley's hand fell on the paper which covered the Derringer; he felt its hard shape beneath his fingers, brushed the paper aside and seized the weapon.

Steve uttered a bellow of rage. "Pull a gun on me, will you!" he cried, and, jerking Horace from the desk, hugged him to him. Neither heeded the man who had come in the front door and now stood at the entrance to the office watching. Back and forth across the floor they struggled, shuffling, panting, upsetting chairs. Steve had gone berserk; Horace fought for life itself. And suddenly there came the muffled sound of a shot, and Steve released his hold with a throaty gasp. For a moment he stood breast to breast with his father while a little wisp of smoked eddied ceilingward; then he collapsed like a wet rag, leaving the lawyer with the gun in his hand looking down at him with horror-stricken eyes.

"Stevie!" cried Horace, and there was that in the cry which tore at Barry Weston's heart strings. "Stevie! My boy! Oh, what have I done?"

He dropped to his knees and gathered his son in his arms. "Stevie!" he cried brokenly, the tears streaming down his face. "Stevie, answer me! I didn't meant to do it! I swear I didn't!"

Through the outer doorway came several men, Matt Billings in the lead. He ran past Barry, stopped at the sight which greeted his eyes. Horace was still supporting Steve, his tears falling on the dead face.

Slowly Matt stopped and picked up the gun. He felt the warm barrel, sniffed the fumes which issued from the weapon.

"So it's murder this time," he said quietly. "And your own son."

The lawyer raised his grief-stricken face and looked

dumbly about him. For an instant he appeared on the verge of speaking, then he lowered his head and sobbed. He had not seen Barry; perhaps it occurred to him then that he, who had always been careful to eliminate witnesses to his acts, had at last jeopardized his life for the need of one.

Certainly the thought struck Barry with all its ironical force. If he remained silent, Moley must hang. Certainly the man deserved hanging; but that heart-broken cry, the agony in Moley's eyes, had touched him to the quick.

He stepped forward. "An accident, Matt. I saw it all. Steve came in drunk and started to quarrel. He tried to choke his father, and Horace grabbed the gun from the desk. It was fired while they were strugglin'. He didn't mean to do it."

Somebody called a doctor, and Horace was persuaded to leave the body. He seemed to know that there was no hope, and sat with his head bowed in his hands while the brief examination was made.

"Dead," pronounced the doctor quietly. "I'll gather a jury and hold the inquest right here."

Horace Moley refused to testify; but when Barry uttered the words which exonerated him, he looked at Weston long and hard. When it was over he called Barry to him.

"I can't honestly thank you for saving a worthless life," he said dully. "I don't want to live. Everything I strove and worked for is gone; there is nothing now but emptiness. You know why I wanted the Basin. I suppose you have guessed that Frothingham and his bank were established to wreck the ranchers and put the property in my hands."

"Yes. Frothingham told me when he was dying. But I had no witnesses and he was too far gone to sign a confession. Tug murdered him for his money, and we chased Tug into the quicksand. He went down, and the money with him. Had we recovered it we intended to use it to save the Basin ranches."

Moley nodded listlessly. "You're smart, Weston. I feared you from the start. And you're a man. Now leave me, please; I have some things to attend to."

Barry went out quietly. He had intended forcing a confession from the man, or, at the very least, of bargaining with him for the return of the ranches now that they would be of no value to Moley; but somehow he could not force himself to it. The wolf, old and tired and broken, no longer inspired fear or hatred; just pity.

He was standing on the sidewalk outside the office when there came to him the sound of another shot. Apprehensive, he leaped through the doorway and into the office. Moley lay sprawled across the desk, the Derringer clutched in his left hand. Before him were spread six deeds conveying back to their original owners the six Basin ranches. There were no witnesses to his signature, but in his right hand he still gripped the pen with which he had signed them, and the ink was not yet dry.

CHAPTER XX

THE LAST VERSE

ONCE more Barry Weston rode to the Cinch-buckle. He rode swiftly, with a smile of anticipation on his face. Jefferson Hope and Harry Webb were still in Mescal, and to them and the delighted Matt Billings he had delivered the deeds which once more made the Basin ranches theirs. That of George Brent he had mailed to Sheridan, Wyoming.

His first visit had been to the Flying W. There, with his bright-eyed mother, his repentant step-father, and Lola and Nip as an audience, he related the dramatic story which closed the struggle for the Basin. His mother cried a little, then, unassisted, got up from her chair and declared that she was completely well.

Lola and Nip walked with him to the door.

"An' now," said Lola bravely, "you weel go to Barbara an' tell her the good news, no? An' she weel be ver' 'appy, an' eef you do not tak her in your arms an' tell her you lof her, you are one great beeg fool. Ees not so, Neep?"

"That's whatever!" seconded Nip. He would have

said the same thing had she declared it was the moon and not the sun which was shining.

They watched him ride away, erect in his saddle, confident, smiling; then Lola turned, her eyes misty. "Oh, Neep!" she cried, and his arms closed about her.

"Here's right where you stay," said Nip firmly. "It's where you belong, honey. Ah, Lola, I love you so much! I won't go far on looks, but I can work, and I sure will work like a son-of-a-gun for you. Lola, I want you to marry me."

She looked up in amazement, starry-eyed. "You would marry—*me?*"

"Nobody else in the whole danged world," declared Nip soberly. "Lola, I want you so much! That first night at the Palace I loved you."

For a short space she looked up into his face and read there only humble devotion, honest love, and a very great tenderness.

Her eyes melted, the soft lips curved. "Ah, Neep! Eef you can be content weeth w'at ees lef' of me, I would be so 'appy to marry you!"

And Nip, with a great cry, drew her close.

Barry dismounted outside the Cinchbuckle ranch house and leaped up the steps. Without knocking he ran into the living room. The place has been dismantled and Barbara was perched on a trunk which Clay strove to latch. They glanced up at his entrance.

"Hello, Barry," said Clay. "You look happy."

"I'm good news personified. Run your eye over that!"

They looked at the paper he handed them. "Why,

it's a deed to the Cinchbuckle!" cried Barbara. "Barry, how did you do it?"

He sat on the trunk beside her and told them the whole story.

"So he killed his own son," said Barbara sadly. "How pitiful."

"And yet it's a fittin' conclusion to the whole sorry mess," said Clay. "I pity the man, but when we think of the hearts he broke and the lives he had snuffed out it seems the only proper end for the old lobo. . . . Say, I'm goin' to hunt up Clement. Tuck came after him this mornin' and dragged him out to that south line cabin. I just got to tell him the news."

He left Barbara and Barry seated on the trunk. The girl's eyes were averted. "And now that you've won the Flying W back," she said softly, "I suppose you will be urging Lola to share it with you."

"Lola?" He was surprised.

"Yes. I didn't intend to spy, Barry, but that day I came back for my quirt I saw you on your knees beside her. You were holding her hand and the expression on your face was—was—well—" She faltered to a stop.

Barry reached out and took one of her hands in his. "The expression on my face was one of eternal gratitude, Barbara; for Lola had just told me that you cared for me." The girl beside him started and tried to withdraw her hand, but he held it firmly.

"And her last words when I left the Flyin' W a short while ago were to the effect that if I didn't take you in my arms and tell you I love you, I would be a very great fool."

"Barry!" He could see the color rise in her cheek.

"And so, not wishin' to be a very great fool, I must tell you, dear, that I've loved you from the time we were kids. All the five lonely years I spent in Montana I kept yearnin' for you. I reckon I've always loved you. But when I came back and saw you—saw how beautiful and sweet and desirable you'd grown—well, I was just tongue-tied. Somehow I didn't feel worthy."

She turned to him then, eyes very bright, the roses in her cheeks.

"Not worthy! Oh, Barry, after all you've done how can you say that! It is I who am unworthy! Oh, if you had only known the hours I thought of you while you were gone! It was your fighting for me that sent you away; and when you returned, you fought for me again."

It was then that he remembered the rest of Lola's advice. He put his arms about her, and there, on the trunk, they whispered to each other the old, old story that to lovers is forever new.

Here on the trunk Clement and Clay and Tuck found them. They rode their horses to the gallery and came trooping into the room. Clay's eyes were bright and he was grinning from ear to ear.

"Barry! Barbara! Oh, what news! Tell 'em, Tuck, before I bust."

Tuck grinned. "Well, the fact is, Barry, that Nip and me done pulled a little trick on you. You know that oil barrel Steve Moley uncovered? Well, Tom Slater didn't bury it there at all."

"Slater didn't—! Tuck, what are you talkin' about?"

"No, he didn't. That day you started out to look for Chet Lewis, me and Nip sat there tryin' to figger out some way that Slater could have cheated old man Moley. We finally decided that he might 'a' buried a barrel of oil and let it seep into the pond, so we went lookin' around. But there wasn't any barrel; that there seepage sure seemed natural enough. We was mighty disappointed at first, but we got to thinkin' that just because Slater hadn't buried a barrel filled with oil was no reason for us not buryin' one."

"Tuck!"

"Uh-huh. So we got the wagon and drove to Nogales and bought one filled with oil and also some hose to go with it. Then we planted the danged thing and let Moley dig it up. And son, our bluff worked! He was so crooked hisself that he was more than willin' to believe Slater had rooked him."

"Tuck, you danged old sidewinder! Then there is oil in the Basin?"

"Barry, it sure looks like it. Me and Clement have been pokin' around, and all the indications are there. I shouldn't be su-prised to see every rancher in the Basin turn out to be a millionaire."

The news was so astounding that for the time there was silence; then to their ears came the sound of a voice raised in song. Tuck went to the door and looked out.

"It's Nip and Lola, and—yeah! your mother and

step-father in a buckboard. Listen! Nip done writ another verse to that song of ours."

Faintly the words reached them:

> *"Oh, I onct loved Lola Gonzales,*
>   *My gosh, but I loved that gal!*
>   *We was married way down at Nogales,*
>   *And settled for life in Mescal."*

As the significance of the words reached Tuck, his face became a study in surprise and dismay. "He's gone and done it! Busted a partnership of ten years standin'! Yes, sir, that's the last verse to the song. Oh, my gosh!" Suddenly he turned and hurried through the doorway.

"Where you goin'?" called Barry after him.

Tuck answered over his shoulder. "I ain't lettin' that rannyhan git ahead of me. I'm goin' to ask Lola if she has a sister."